She really wanted to spend more time with him—

About as much as she wanted to slam her hand in a car door. It was more opportunity to say something foolish, something he'd laugh about. She was still squirming over the things she'd said earlier, making it sound as if just *thinking* about sex was a terrible sin.

Libby thought about sex.

She thought about it a lot.

Actually sometimes sex was all she could think of…. But she wanted it to be with someone she loved, who loved her, someone who wanted to hold her during the night instead of calculating the fastest way out the door the minute his breathing slowed.

That someone wasn't Neil O'Rourke.

Dear Reader,

I've put together a list of Silhouette Romance New Year's resolutions to help you get off to a great start in 2004!

- Play along with our favorite boss's daughter's mischievous, matchmaking high jinks. In *Rules of Engagement* (#1702) by Carla Cassidy, Emily Winters—aka the love goddess—is hoping to unite a brooding exec and feisty businesswoman. This is the fifth title in Silhouette Romance's exclusive, six-book MARRYING THE BOSS'S DAUGHTER series.

- Enjoy every delightful word of *The Bachelor Boss* (#1703) by the always-popular Julianna Morris. In this modern romantic fairy tale, a prim plain Jane melts the heart of a sexy playboy.

- Join the fun when a cowboy's life is turned inside out by a softhearted beauty and the tiny charge he finds on his doorstep. *Baby, Oh Baby!* (#1704) is the first title in Teresa Southwick's enchanting new three-book miniseries IF WISHES WERE… Stay tuned next month for the next title in this series that features three friends who have their dreams come true in unexpected ways.

- Be sure not to miss *The Baby Chronicles* (#1705) by Lissa Manley. This heartwarming reunion romance is sure to put a satisfied smile on your face.

Have a great New Year!

Mavis C. Allen
Associate Senior Editor

Please address questions and book requests to:
Silhouette Reader Service
U.S.: 3010 Walden Ave., P.O. Box 1325, Buffalo, NY 14269
Canadian: P.O. Box 609, Fort Erie, Ont. L2A 5X3

The Bachelor Boss

JULIANNA MORRIS

SILHOUETTE *Romance*®

Published by Silhouette Books

America's Publisher of Contemporary Romance

With thanks to Rick and Sheila

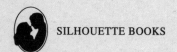 SILHOUETTE BOOKS

ISBN 0-373-19703-9

THE BACHELOR BOSS

Visit Silhouette at www.eHarlequin.com

Printed in U.S.A.

JULIANNA MORRIS

has an offbeat sense of humor, which frequently gets her into trouble. She is often accused of being curious about everything…her interests ranging from oceanography and photography to traveling, antiquing, walking on the beach and reading science fiction.

Julianna loves cats of all shapes and sizes, and recently she was adopted by a feline companion named Merlin. Like his namesake, Merlin is an alchemist—she says he can transform the house into a disaster area in nothing flat. And since he shares the premises with a writer, it's interesting to note that he's particularly fond of knocking books onto the floor.

Julianna happily reports meeting Mr. Right. Together they are working on a new dream of building a shoreline home in the Great Lakes area.

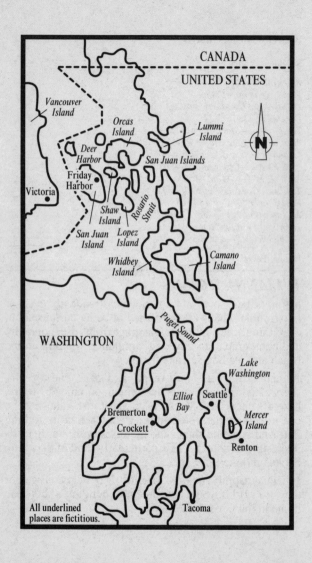

CANADA

UNITED STATES

Vancouver Island

Orcas Island

Lummi Island

N

Deer Harbor

San Juan Islands

Friday Harbor

Rosario Strait

Victoria

Shaw Island

Lopez Island

San Juan Island

Whidbey Island

Camano Island

Puget Sound

WASHINGTON

Lake Washington

Elliot Bay

Seattle

Bremerton

Mercer Island

Crockett

Renton

Tacoma

All underlined places are fictitious.

Chapter One

"Well, if it isn't Miss Dumont," said a voice from the open office door.

Libby groaned silently.

Neil O'Rourke.

Her least favorite person in the world. Until now she'd been having a really good day. What made it worse was that her first instinct was to check her appearance in a mirror—Neil had that effect on women, being as revoltingly handsome as he was obnoxious.

"Did you need something, Mr. O'Rourke?" she asked politely. As much as she didn't like him, he *was* Kane O'Rourke's brother, and Kane was the owner and founder of the company, so it didn't make sense to be rude.

"Yes. And don't you think it's time you dropped the 'Mr. O'Rourke' routine?" Neil asked.

Libby's eyes narrowed. "No. We barely know each other."

His smile irritated her even more, mostly because it was Neil. "I wouldn't exactly say *that*," he said.

Drat the man.

Yet even as Libby fumed, she squirmed at the reminder of a long ago night when she'd been young and foolishly flattered that a man like Neil O'Rourke had asked her out on a date. She'd never forget breaking away from their out-of-control kiss, pulling her clothes together…her heart pounding because she wasn't certain that pulling her clothes together was what she really wanted. Fighting the urge to be just a little bad.

Yeah, that pretty much covered it.

He'd gotten his arrogant masculine nose out of joint, she'd acted like a prig, and everything went downhill from there.

Of course, the only reason he remembered that evening was because she was probably one of the few members of the female sex who'd ever said no to him. She'd seen happily married women blush and sigh at his careless smile.

"I have a lot of work to do," Libby said pointedly, hoping he'd take the hint and leave.

"So do I, but Kane wants to see us both in his office. Maybe he's going on a second honeymoon and wants us to work together again."

She wrinkled her nose. When Kane had met Beth and gotten married he'd asked Neil to run the company during his absence—much to her consternation. The man was impossible. She'd heaved a sigh of relief when he returned to the international branch, because she didn't have to see or think about him there.

"I'm not Kane's executive assistant any longer."

His grin was faintly wicked. "That's right. I keep forgetting you're the administrative officer now."

Huh.

Neil never forgot anything, especially how to annoy the living daylights out of her. Of course, being annoying must be a natural talent since he didn't know her well enough to understand which buttons to push.

"Shall we go?" he murmured.

Libby stayed silent as they walked the short distance to the CEO's office, resisting the urge to smooth her hair and make sure her blouse was tucked into the waistband of her skirt. Feminine vanity had a habit of rearing its head around Neil, no matter how hard she fought it.

"Hey, bro," Neil said as they walked into Kane's inner sanctum.

"Hey." Kane smiled and waited until they were seated, then leaned forward. "Libby, you're aware that I'm delegating authority in the company so I have more time to spend with Beth." He beamed at his wife's name. "As part of the reorganization I've named Neil as the president of the New Business Developments division. I told him about it earlier."

"That's...nice," she murmured.

"Yes, but what he hasn't heard is that I'm appointing you as his vice president. I wanted you both to be here for the news."

Libby's heart lodged in her throat.

"What?" she demanded in unison with Neil. She looked at him and was glad to see he appeared as thunderstruck as she felt.

Kane lifted his shoulders in a small shrug. "I realize you haven't always gotten along, but you have skills that complement each other, and you managed to work together earlier this year.'' He shot a look at his brother. ''You'll find Libby's abilities are just what you need.''

She blinked, torn between shock and hysteria.

This couldn't be happening. She couldn't possibly be Neil O'Rourke's vice president. He was too...*everything.* The two brothers were nearly identical in appearance, though Neil had cool gray eyes in contrast to Kane's blue. Both were high-powered and driven for success, but Kane managed to be kind and friendly, while Neil was distant and impatient.

Darn it all. She'd just gotten rid of the man and now he was back. Wasn't a few weeks working with him enough punishment for one lifetime? It wasn't that she didn't want the new position. Being promoted so quickly might be a little unconventional, but Kane never did things in the usual way. And since he'd built O'Rourke Enterprises into a multibillion-dollar corporation, people usually had the good sense to agree with his wishes.

Still, how could she work with someone so *impossible?*

Libby sneaked a glance at the impossible man in question and saw he didn't look any happier than she felt.

Well, fine.

Let *him* be the one to tell Kane it was out of the question.

''Libby?'' Kane prompted.

''Uh...that's wonderful,'' she said, lying through her teeth.

''You've earned it. I'm still working out the final details, but I've decided to have each of my division presidents and vice presidents directly involved in a project together in order to build teamwork.''

Neil cleared his throat. ''That's an interesting idea, but we'll be busy with our own duties.''

''And one of those duties will be cooperating on a project together.''

Libby recognized the expression on her boss's face, even if his brother didn't. Kane had mentioned his plans, but she hadn't thought much about it other than sparing a moment of sympathy for the poor sap who ended up working with Neil O'Rourke. Before his short stint in the CEO's office she'd avoided Neil for nebulous reasons she'd never really thought about. Now she actively disliked him.

''What project are you thinking about?'' she asked.

''The bed-and-breakfast inn proposal.'' Kane handed her the file. ''You were particularly interested in it, so I thought it would be the perfect place to start your collaboration.''

Lord, Kane should never have picked something so homey and small scale if he hoped to get Neil excited. Neil loved glitz and glamour, the fast pace of international wheeling and dealing and high finance. He was a brilliant maverick. Developing a line of historic bed-and-breakfast inns was the last thing he'd want to do.

''B and B's?'' Neil sounded predictably appalled, as if he'd just been asked to work on a line of brothels. ''I think that's a project Libby could handle on her own.''

Kane shook his head. ''I want both of you involved. This is Beth's idea, and it goes at the top of the list.''

Beth.

Kane's wife.

The magic word.

A warm smile crossed Neil's face, so apparently he was fond of his new sister-in-law. "Beth does love old places. We'll make it our first priority."

"Good. The two of you can go over the proposal this afternoon. You'll have until after Christmas to get things moving on it before we start the formal reorganization."

Libby's fingers tightened on the file. She'd worked on putting the proposal together and had hoped to be assigned to the project, but this wasn't what she'd had in mind.

"*Today?*" Neil asked. He cast her a sideways glance that made her squirm.

What was it about him that made her so…aware?

"Today," Kane said firmly.

Libby edged toward the door. "In that case, I've got a lot to do in the meantime. Thanks again, Kane."

"No thanks are necessary. Your contract will be ready in a few days, along with a generous salary boost. You'll always have a place with us, Libby." From years of working with Kane, Libby knew he was reassuring her that no matter how things turned out with Neil, her place with the company was guaranteed.

"That's nice to hear." She forced herself to leave at a dignified pace, only to have Neil follow her.

"It isn't afternoon yet," she snapped. As a rule she tried to be calmly courteous with him, but Kane's announcement had scrambled her brains worse than an eggbeater.

"Now is as good a time as any. Kane likes the teamwork approach, remember?"

Libby practically snorted. Neil O'Rourke wasn't a team player. He enjoyed being in charge too much for that. Thankfully, except for his brief time as acting CEO, she'd hardly seen him over the years. He'd traveled all over the world for the company, earning a reputation as a tough and able negotiator.

Too bad he wasn't better with people. She wasn't the only employee who avoided him; his cool direct gaze could cut right through a person.

"A leopard can't change his spots," she muttered, not that he'd understand. Neil honestly didn't seem to know he had the corporate persona of a runaway locomotive, mashing everyone in his path. Kane was indulging in wishful thinking if he thought his brother would listen to anyone on how to run the new division, much less to her.

Maybe Neil was different with his family.

Maybe.

She was acquainted with two of his sisters, Shannon and Kathleen, and thought his mother was a lovely woman, but Neil was a puzzle beyond words.

A small frown creased his forehead. "What is that supposed to mean?"

"Oh, come on. Teamwork? You?"

The note of amused disbelief in Libby's voice irritated Neil. He knew it was his fault they didn't get along—he'd acted like an oversexed jock on the one date they'd had years ago. A naive preacher's daughter and a former college football star weren't a good mix. People who thought that all preacher's daughters were wild as sin didn't know anything. Jeez, she was practically a nun.

Yet he didn't dislike Libby, he just didn't think she was vice president material. She was too softhearted, an innocent with the cutthroat business sense of a newborn kitten.

"You can't know how I feel about teamwork," he said slowly.

"I have a pretty good idea."

His eyebrows shot upward. "I don't think a single date gives you that much insight to my character. Especially since we've hardly said 'boo' to each other ever since."

It was the first time since that disastrous night the subject had been directly raised, and relief crept through him. They should have cleared the air a long time ago instead of just going their own way and avoiding contact.

Hell, he probably wouldn't have thought about it again if she hadn't been so damned desirable…and so very prudish with her sexy little body. If he'd learned nothing else, it was that dating co-workers was a lousy idea.

"Maybe, but it *was* instructive," she snapped. Her green eyes were stormy and Neil restrained a grin. This was an interesting side to Libby; he wanted to see more. It was like watching the kitten discover she had claws.

"That was a date, this is business," he said.

"I've heard about the way you work. And I saw it for myself when you were in the CEO's office. You obviously have to be in control, no matter what."

"Isn't that what we all want?" he asked.

She made a disgusted gesture. "Not all of us have a fetish about it. You must be ready to chew nails over Kane making me a vice president."

Neil wasn't thrilled, but he'd never admit it to Libby. And since he planned to make the New Developments division the most successful in the company, he would have to deal with her one way or another. Besides, it could be a lot of fun teasing that pink color into her cheeks.

"Especially with me being a woman," Libby added.

"What?" He scowled, no longer amused. "I don't have a problem with qualified women in business, so don't put words into my mouth."

"Ah, but you don't think I'm qualified."

"That remains to be seen. Your qualifications, that is," Neil said, giving her a measuring glance. Libby certainly looked the part of a career woman...*now*. But the day they met she'd been wearing an unstructured sweater and skirt.

That damned bulky sweater should have been his first clue, he thought irritably. It had practically screamed small-town innocent, but even the most sophisticated women had been wearing the down-home earthy look back then. If he'd known she was a naive virgin he would have stayed a thousand miles away.

"I'm sure you'll do a fine job," he said, distracted by the memory. Or was it the memory of sweet curves that fitted perfectly against him?

Damn. Where had that come from? Libby had a fine body—not that she did anything to advertise it—but he'd been with his share of gorgeous women. *Willing* women who didn't have marriage and a baby carriage on the mind.

"Marriage and a baby carriage? What do you mean by that?" Libby demanded.

Neil winced, realizing he'd muttered the last part aloud. "Er...I was thinking about Kane," he said.

"He's turned into a huge advocate of marriage and children ever since he met Beth."

"Is that so terrible?"

"Depends on how you see it. I think it must be hard to keep your focus while at the same time dealing with a nagging spouse and kids."

"You mean a nagging *wife*. But for your information, not all wives nag," Libby shot back, though she didn't know why she bothered. Neil's views on the incompatibility of marriage and business were infamous.

"I just meant…" He shrugged. "Forget it. I guess marriage is all right for other people."

"Wow. Isn't that big of you."

Neil looked surprised by her sarcastic tone, and to be honest, Libby was surprised herself. She'd never spoken her mind to him, not since that embarrassing night when she'd said all sorts of things about men who expected to sleep with a woman on the first date.

She sighed, a hollow feeling in her tummy.

Principles were fine things, but she was awfully tired of going home to a lonely house in the evening.

"I'm not going to hold anything against an executive who wants to get married, if that's what you think."

Libby rolled her eyes. "As if your brother would let you."

Neil regarded her curiously. "You think Kane and I are that different?"

"Like night and day."

"Because he got married."

"No." She shook her head in exasperation. "Because he's nice, and you're…" Libby stopped, realizing if she'd sounded rude before, it would be nothing to calling him a smug, self-centered chauvinist with the compassion of a fence post.

Swallowing, she dropped into the chair behind her desk. He couldn't seem to understand that the people who worked for O'Rourke Enterprises were people, not machines, with lives outside the company that were important to them.

"I'm what?"

The small twitch to Neil's mouth suggested he had a good idea of what she'd almost called him. He sat on a chair himself and stretched out his legs. From head to toe he was the consummate executive—from his expensive suit to his ice-blue silk shirt and perfect tie. There was only one time she'd ever seen him in a less than immaculate state, and that was the night they'd almost...

She put a hasty brake on her thoughts. Okay, Neil could be charming when he wanted something, and he'd come *very* close to getting what he'd once wanted from her. It didn't mean anything.

"Well?" he prompted. "What am I?"

"You're just...different."

"Different, as in 'not nice.'"

"I didn't say that," she said, annoyed.

"You didn't have to." Neil told himself he should stop. This wasn't the right way to start their new relationship as president and vice president, but he didn't want to work with veiled hostility simmering between them—he'd take open warfare over that. For that matter, conflict could be very good for business.

"You said not to put words in your mouth, so don't do it with me."

Yet her cheeks pinkened, and he knew she felt

guilty for whatever she'd been thinking—which just proved she hadn't changed over the years.

Sweet.

Innocent.

With an interesting streak of temper. Rather like her hair, a rich silky brown with hints of hidden fire— it was still long, caught back in an attractive French braid, though small tendrils had escaped and framed her face.

Neil shifted in the chair. He didn't have any business thinking her temper was interesting or not. Libby was off-limits. Of course, that didn't mean he couldn't enjoy the situation.

''Are you thinking about tying the knot, and are afraid my beliefs about marriage will be a problem?'' he asked. ''The company policy is clear—we're a family-friendly business. So you have nothing to be concerned about, no matter what my personal feelings are on the issue.''

Libby stared in astonishment and he cursed his wayward tongue. He really hadn't thought that much about her over the years, but now that she was going to be his vice president, all sorts of questions were banging around in his head.

Most of them were none of his concern.

And he certainly shouldn't be wondering if the faint scent of vanilla drifting from her skin was a perfume, or some other bit of unique feminine chemistry. Hell, it wasn't the least bit sophisticated, but on Libby the fragrance was fresh and light, without being cloying.

''No, I'm not thinking about 'tying the knot' as you put it,'' she said. ''I hate that phrase. It makes marriage sound like prison or some other type of captivity. Do you think Kane feels that way about being married to Beth?''

"Of course not.''

"Then let's drop the subject. We're supposed to be talking about the B and B proposal, remember?''

He remembered.

He rarely thought about anything *but* business, though his mother was doing her best to distract him with introductions to "nice young women.'' Nice *single* women, of course. Having finally gotten two of her sons married, she wanted to see all her children taking a trip down the proverbial aisle, followed a few months later with the announcement that a baby was on the way.

Libby pulled a pen and pad of paper from a drawer. "How do you want to get started?''

"Give me a quick rundown on the project.''

She kept her spine straight, barely skimming the back of her chair. "The first active steps will be choosing sites and contacting historical societies for local history and background.''

"What?'' Neil rocked forward in his chair. "We have to deal with hysterical societies?''

"That's *historical* societies,'' Libby corrected, the corners of her mouth twitching despite herself. Historical societies could be very passionate about their work, but she liked working with people who cared. "Of course we'll have to talk with them, and consult with restoration experts and contractors. By the way, we should use local people as much as possible as part of the community development aspect of the project.''

He grimaced without looking particularly upset. "You mean we'll be restoring old buildings that should have been demolished decades ago. I don't suppose we could buy a bunch of existing bed-and-breakfast inns and slap our name on them?'' he asked, a rueful humor in his voice.

She barely kept from rolling her eyes. Neil was so focused on the future, he couldn't see the benefit to saving wonderful old survivors from the past.

Modern, that defined Neil O'Rourke.

Glitz, high finance, his world moving at lightning speed. If he went on vacation it was to five-star hotels in the most exotic and glamorous places, so bed-and-breakfast inns weren't likely to interest him. He avoided ties that might slow him down—like a wife and children. The idea of spending a quiet evening at home would probably horrify him.

''I don't suppose we can.'' Libby handed him the file. ''Why don't you go over this on your own? I'll come by your office at one this afternoon so we can discuss it.'' Without waiting for acknowledgment, she headed for the door and stood by it, making it obvious she expected him to leave.

''Libby…''

She looked at his handsome face, and the same old shiver went through her tummy. Why did she have to be attracted to him? Wasn't attraction supposed to be based on respect and liking, more than chemistry? She didn't know Neil that well, but she *didn't* like him, so it wasn't logical the way her body responded whenever he walked into the room.

''Yes?''

''We should talk about what happened eleven years ago. Get everything said and out in the open.''

Her pulse surged. ''That isn't such a good idea.''

"Why not? Haven't you wondered what would have happened if we hadn't stopped that night?"

Only about a million times.

Not that it would have made any difference. According to the office gossip she couldn't avoid, Neil's idea of a long term relationship was a weekend in the Bahamas.

"There isn't any point in discussing it," she said.

"It's getting in the way of us working together."

"No, it isn't," Libby said.

It was true.

Their disastrous date, embarrassing as the memory might be, wasn't the real reason they didn't get along.

"Then what's the problem?" Neil's gray eyes had darkened, and his gaze moved deliberately over her. "Is it because I called you the virgin queen? I've never apologized for that, and I am sorry."

He sounded sincere and Libby couldn't control the flush rising in her cheeks...or the instinctive warmth sliding through her veins. "That has nothing to do with it. There are lots of reasons we don't get along, but it's mostly because we're poles apart in the way we look at life."

Because I'm a small town country girl and you're a big city snob, she added silently. She didn't like cities, fast nightlife, or the high-stakes gambles that Neil O'Rourke thrived upon. Dealing with Neil was like dealing with unstable dynamite—no matter how careful you were, in the end you got burned.

"Maybe. But there's still an attraction between us."

"I'm not attracted to you," she denied instantly. "And if you're attracted to me, it's only because I said no. If we'd slept together I would have been old news before the week was out. You have the staying power of an amoeba.''

''Really? I'm told I have more stamina than most men.'' His tone was so outrageously suggestive she wanted to scream.

''And like most men, all you ever think about is sex. If you ever had an honest-to-God tender emotion for a woman, I think you'd jump off a building just to get rid of it. Now get out.'' Libby slammed the door behind him and stormed back to her desk.

Men.

They were the rottenest, most unreasonable creatures imaginable. She didn't know why a woman would bother with them, except they were necessary to keep the human race going.

Chapter Two

Neil couldn't keep a grin from splitting his face as he strode away.

Libby might be an innocent, but that unexpected temper was priceless. Of course, he shouldn't have said he was still attracted to her. It just made things more complicated, but it was entertaining watching her blush and react so strongly.

No matter what she claimed, he wasn't attracted to her just because she'd refused him. Absolutely not. He had his moments he wasn't proud of, but he wasn't *that* shallow and immature. He could keep things under control without actually doing anything about it.

"Any messages?" he asked his secretary.

"They're on your desk, Mr. O'Rourke." Margie turned back to her desk, avoiding his gaze.

He hesitated. "Is something wrong?"

"No, of course not."

Neil waited, then decided not to say anything else.

She was new and apparently having personal troubles, but he didn't want to make either of them uncomfortable by asking too much.

"Thank you. I have an appointment with Libby Dumont at one this afternoon. Keep my schedule clear."

"Yes, sir."

Going into his office, he tossed the bed-and-breakfast file on his desk. "B and B's," he murmured, shaking his head as he swiftly scanned the pages.

After several hours of making notes and jotting down figures, Neil got up and stretched, realizing he'd worked through lunch again. He had to admit the bed-and-breakfast project had some interesting aspects, but what still boggled his mind was that Kane had promoted Libby Dumont. Vice president? She might be all right in a division that handled corporate giving, but new developments?

His brother was going soft in the head. Beth was a great wife and sister-in-law, but if that's what falling in love did to you, the rest of the world could keep it.

Love did strange things to people.

Restless all at once, Neil paced around the room, then stood at the window and looked out at the Puget Sound. It was a rare, cloudless day in Seattle, the sun shining brightly on the water. A ferry chugged away from the shore, with seagulls soaring and swooping in the air above.

He usually tried not to think about how his father had given up the work he cherished—handcrafting fine wood furniture—to take a higher paying job in the forest industry. A job that eventually killed him, just to support a growing family.

There were too many tradeoffs to love and marriage, and Neil knew he was too selfish to make them. It was better to be honest with himself, than to get married and end up in a bitter divorce, making everyone miserable.

The phone on the desk rang. It was Margie, telling him that Libby was waiting for their appointment.

"Tell her to come in."

Libby walked inside with an I'm-going-to-be-nice-to-the-jackass-if-it-kills-me expression on her face.

"Good afternoon, Mr. O'Rourke."

He looked at her narrowly. That "Mr. O'Rourke" nonsense would have to end. Sooner or later he'd get her to call him Neil. It was a challenge, and he loved challenges.

"Good afternoon, Miss Dumont," he mimicked back. "You do know my first name, don't you?"

"Of course," she said evenly.

"Then use it."

"I'm not the only employee who calls you Mr. O'Rourke," Libby murmured.

Neil frowned. Come to think of it, she was right.

"But just your subordinates," she added. "So you have nothing to worry about. I mean, it's a little stuffy, but who cares when you're in charge, right?"

"I'm not a snob, Libby. I've never insisted on that kind of formality," he said, stung.

"But you've never invited us peons to call you Neil, either."

"I did this morning and it didn't do any good. You still insist on using Mr. O'Rourke," Neil snapped.

"And nobody's a peon at O'Rourke Enterprises. You damn well know that."

Libby took a breath. She couldn't believe she'd let her tongue run away with her that morning, and now she was doing it again. After a lifetime of being a well-behaved preacher's daughter, watching what she said and trying to be tactful no matter what the situation, she'd totally lost it.

Of course, by all accounts, *tact* wasn't high on Neil O'Rourke's list of priorities.

"Maybe we should just talk about the B and B proposal," she said quickly.

"Suits me. Where do you think we should start looking for properties? I've made some notes, but I should hear your ideas about it before we go ahead."

Libby wanted to say Endicott, her hometown. If a community ever needed development, it was Endicott. But that would convince him more than ever that she was too sentimental to be "executive" material.

"We could write various historical societies and ask if they know of any likely houses that would meet our purpose," she suggested instead.

Neil shook his head. "It's bad enough we have to talk to them at all, but you'll get them up in arms before we even start," he declared.

"They might decide to work with us, you know. For the chance of saving a piece of history."

"Sure, and I believe in leprechauns."

Libby doubted Neil had ever believed in something so whimsical, even as a boy.

"Do you have a better suggestion?" she asked.

"Yes. We could assign a team to scout locations. Other teams can work on acquisitions and restoration."

Her chin lifted. "Well, that certainly has the personal touch Kane and Beth have in mind for the project."

Neil glared. "Fine, then we'll do it together. *All* of it. The two of us, every step of the way. That should have a personal enough touch to suit you."

Swell.

She really wanted to spend more time with him—about as much as she wanted to slam her hand in a car door. It was more opportunity to say something foolish, something he'd laugh about. She was still squirming over the things she'd said earlier, making it sound as if just *thinking* about sex was a terrible sin.

Libby thought about sex.

She thought about it a lot.

Actually, sometimes sex was all she could think of, though she usually tried to blame it on hormones and being that time of the month. But she wanted to be with someone she loved, who loved her, someone who wanted to hold her during the night instead of calculating the fastest way out the door the minute his breathing slowed.

That someone wasn't Neil O'Rourke.

He wanted success, power, and a life of travel and accomplishment, equating marriage to sacrifice. *Sacrifice.* No woman in her right mind wanted a man who considered her a sacrifice, no matter how good-looking he might be. It wasn't worth the heartache.

And she didn't even know why she was thinking about it except she'd never reacted to any man more strongly than Neil.

Blast.

It wasn't fair that he could turn her inside out without even knowing he'd done it. She'd gone for months at a time without thinking about the man, and then only in passing, but now her head was filled with wayward thoughts.

Maybe it was knowing he wasn't going anywhere. This time she was stuck with him.

"A historical bed-and-breakfast line wasn't my idea," she said, trying to sound calm. "You don't have to be annoyed with me for wanting to do things the way Kane asked."

"Whatever. Just stay here," Neil ordered, getting up and stomping out.

"Stay?" Libby scowled at his empty chair.

She wasn't a golden retriever he could order to stay put. Then she shrugged, deciding she'd have to pick her battles carefully when it came to Neil. Otherwise she'd never stop arguing with the man, being as he was the most annoying person on the planet.

After a few minutes he returned with a load of phone books in his arms.

"I got these from the secretarial pool," he said, dropping them in a heap on the couch. "We'll go through them and start making calls to real estate agents about likely properties.

Libby lifted one of the dog-eared phone books in disbelief. The thing was eight years old. Hadn't Neil ever heard of the Internet? The information highway loaded with helpful items like up-to-date phone numbers? He must have dug these out of a back cabinet somebody had forgotten.

A bubble of laughter struggled for release in her throat.

He had to be totally rattled, beyond thinking clearly. They hadn't even talked about what towns to start in, but his first course of action was to bring in some ancient phone books and randomly start contacting real estate agents?

"Start calling," Neil said. "That's a separate phone line over by the couch."

Within seconds he was talking to an agent, crisply barking out his "needs" and asking that a list of suitable properties be faxed immediately.

She followed suit, glancing at him from time to time, and realizing that maybe his plan wasn't daft after all. It could be more organized, but at least it had a personal touch.

At one point Neil smiled so warmly that Libby was startled. Then her gaze narrowed. From the bits of conversation she could catch, he was obviously talking to a woman who was doing her best to flirt.

What about his precious professionalism?

Why did she care?

Libby hastily looked back at her own phone book. It didn't sound like he was flirting back with "Sue," but he was such a stickler for being cool and professional she'd have expected him to end the conversation with the first calculated giggle.

"How many agents have you talked to?" he asked after another hour.

She counted. "Eight who promised to fax something today."

"I've got fifteen. Let's see if anything has come in, and we can decide which properties we're going to look at first." He picked up the phone. "Margie? Yes, I know a lot is coming in on the machine. Bring it in."

Margie sidled into the office like a frightened rabbit and handed Neil a stack of paper. Libby gave her an encouraging smile before she left, recognizing the sign of fresh tears on the other woman's face.

Neil didn't even look up and Libby wanted to kick him. Granted, Margie was new to working in an executive suite, but she'd been with the company for a long while and she was going through a tough time with a sick daughter. A little sensitivity from her equally new boss would help.

"Looks like some good stuff to start with," Neil muttered, sitting next to Libby on the couch, and flipping through the faxed sheets.

He recognized the ones from the agents he'd talked with. They were adequate, but Libby's faxes were much longer, provided more material, and the cover sheets contained hand-written notes saying things like "enjoyed talking with you," "anything we can do to help," and "sounds like a great project, love to be a part of it."

The only personal note to him was a message from Susan Weston, who asked if he wanted to have dinner the next time he was in Olympia.

"Olympia?" Libby asked, looking over his shoulder at the boldly scrawled invitation. "It's a beautiful city, but I thought the idea was to look for places in small towns, especially towns needing revitalization."

"It is." Neil crumpled the sheet and tossed it on the floor, unaccountably embarrassed. He hadn't encouraged Sue to flirt. He'd dealt with her before on land deals in the south Puget sound area, so had naturally called her to see if she had any likely listings for a bed-and-breakfast inn. "Susan has a big agency. She lists property from Lacey to Aberdeen."

"Oh. Personal friend?"

"No." The denial came out more sharply than he'd intend. "We've done business before, that's all."

Libby squirmed on the soft leather cushions, trying to sit up straight, and her leg brushed his thigh.

Damn. He should never have thought about her curves, her perfume, or anything else so personal. They worked together, for pity's sake. She was his vice president. And if she was the reason he was so fierce about not dating someone in the company, then so what?

They'd had one date, eleven years ago. A date that ended with him taking a cold shower.

"Er...Libby," Neil murmured, hoping she'd sit still and quit turning him on. Hell, he was in charge here.

"What?"

"About this morning—I meant you were attractive. Not that I was interested in starting something."

"I see." Her eyes darkened stormily. "Well, let *me* be clear. I'm not interested in starting something, either."

Great.

They were both on the same page.

Of course, he'd ticked her off again, but hadn't he decided a little conflict would be good for business?

Libby squirmed again, only this time she got to her feet. She tugged at her skirt that had ridden up and made an obvious attempt to compose herself.

"I'll do some Internet research on these listings," she said, color flags high in her cheeks. "Then I'll prepare a preliminary report and you can decide which sites you're going to visit next week."

"The sites *we're* going to visit," Neil reminded. "We're supposed to do this together so we can build teamwork. So we'll drive ourselves rather than take a chauffeur," he said, deciding it would be a good idea to have one of them occupied with driving. Besides, he didn't care for limousines, no matter how convenient.

"Fine. I'll e-mail the report to you later," Libby said, and hurried out.

His private phone rang and he hauled himself off the couch to answer it.

"How is your first day as president going?" asked Kane.

Neil thought about Libby's flashing eyes and the angry color in her cheeks, and decided he shouldn't mention either one. "It's great."

"Good. You remember the party is tonight, right?" Their twin nieces' fourth birthday party was that evening, and they both planned to leave work early.

"Yup. I'm coming."

"Don't forget you're supposed to bring the ice cream."

"Yeah. Strawberry, or something." Neil deliberately sounded vague.

Kane's sigh was exasperated, even over the phone line. "No. Chocolate for Peggy, and vanilla for Amy. Stop by the grocery store on the way. And get lots, you know how they love ice cream."

Neil grinned. After their father's death, Kane had done his best to fill his shoes, quitting college and managing to make a fortune at the same time he was supporting the family. He enjoyed playing big-brother-turned-father-figure so much, they still indulged him every now and then. Of course, he'd probably have his fill of being "daddy" once his wife gave birth to their first baby and he experienced 2:00 a.m. feedings for himself.

"That's right. Thanks for the reminder."

Neil chuckled as he replaced the receiver. He'd enjoyed running O'Rourke Enterprises when Kane was courting and on his honeymoon, but he hadn't expected it to last. Having Kane decide to establish new internal corporate divisions was a boon.

Now with Libby as his vice president...he rubbed the side of his jaw. It was going to be interesting. She had some intriguing qualities he hadn't expected, though whether they would help or hinder him, he didn't know.

The phone rang again and he picked it up, still deep in thought. "O'Rourke, here."

"That sounds so cold, darlin'."

It was his mother.

"Are you calling to remind me about the ice cream? Kane already took care of that."

"Actually I heard about Libby's promotion, and thought you might bring her to the party. I haven't seen the dear child since Kane and Beth's wedding—you know Dylan is coming, and they got on so well at the reception."

Neil groaned. His mom liked Libby Dumont, and she liked the idea of Libby becoming a daughter-in-law even more. She'd worked on him for a while, but when it became obvious that he and Libby were grossly incompatible, she'd decided his younger brother, Dylan, was a possibility.

He had news...Dylan had no more interest in finding a bride than *he* did.

"Mom, don't you think trying to match Dylan with someone else might upset Katrina?"

"Dylan can't see Kate, either, though she's been standin' right in front of him for years." Pegeen sounded quite put out, because Katrina Douglas was another name on her daughter-in-law wish list. "But invite Libby just the same."

"All right." There wasn't any point in arguing, when his mother made up her mind she could teach stubborn to a mule. "I'll see you later."

Neil dropped his head back onto his chair. He'd started the day with a great promotion, then he'd learned his vice president would be Libby Dumont. In just a few hours they'd already had several disagreements, and he'd been painfully reminded that she was still as attractive as ever.

Beautiful, really.

In a fresh-scrubbed sort of way.

And his delightful, very Irish mother was determined to get Libby married to one of her sons, come hell or high water.

Man, was he in trouble.

At four o'clock a new message alert flashed on Neil's computer. He opened the e-mail and found Libby's preliminary report, listing various properties, their historical significance and other pertinent material.

Neil quickly printed the document and hurried out. He walked into Libby's office, and his nerves went on alert. It wasn't that she dressed provocatively. Her trim, dark blue suit accentuated the slender lines of her body without drawing attention to her curves. Problem was, he knew all about her curves and how good they felt beneath his fingers—so good he'd never forgotten it.

She was standing next to her desk, explaining something to a tall, gangly young man who looked familiar for some reason.

"Mr. O'Rourke," the young man exclaimed when he saw Neil. He threw out a nervous hand and knocked over a cup of coffee.

Oh, jeez.

Neil remembered him now. Duncan "Dunk" Anderson. Every time he'd ever seen Dunk he'd managed to spill, break, spindle or mutilate something.

Libby grabbed a handful of tissue and began sopping up the mess. She shot a dire glance in Neil's direction, which seemed patently unfair since it was Dunk who'd spilled the coffee.

"I'm so sorry, Libby. I can't believe I did that."

"It's all right, Duncan," she said calmly. "Why don't you take that material over to Kane? I'll finish up here."

"Sure thing." With another sideways glance at Neil, Dunk scooped a file from a nearby credenza and bolted for the door.

"Please tell me he's only here because there's a flu epidemic and everyone else is desperately ill," Neil muttered.

"Duncan is highly qualified."

"For what? The demolition derby? Oh, God, Dunk is Kane's new executive assistant, isn't he?"

Libby rolled her eyes. "Yes, he is. I recommended him and Kane agreed."

Neil groaned. "Couldn't you have chosen someone better…like Typhoid Mary? Honestly, your employee recommendations could use some help."

"I don't know what you mean." Except Libby *did* know, because a few weeks ago she had hand-picked the employee to replace Neil's latest in a long string of secretaries. She'd had a lot of fun, too, watching him squirm over her selection. Not that it lasted, he'd quickly moved Margie Clarke into the position, instead.

"You know perfectly well what I'm talking about," he snapped.

"Not really. Tami Berkut is intelligent, excellent on the computer, and does great phone. She's highly qualified and very…*willing*. Eager to please in every way."

Neil winced at the subtle dig in Libby's voice. Tami Berkut—also known as Tam Tam the Barracuda—had a fondness for tight red sweaters that showed off her spectacular breasts, and an itch to sleep her way through the executive washroom. But she wasn't a bad employee, so he'd had her reassigned to a fifty-something executive who was devoted to his mother and thoroughly disinterested in red sweaters.

"Anyway, Kane likes Duncan, and he did a great job when I was on vacation a couple years ago. Besides, he's only nervous around *you,* not anyone else. I think it has something to do with that cool, superior stare of yours."

"I don't have a superior stare."

"Could have fooled me."

"I don't." Neil insisted, a little offended. First she'd implied he was a snob, now he was cool and superior.

He didn't think he was better than anyone else. Okay, he should admit preferring more office ceremony than Kane. But Kane could afford to be relaxed—he *owned* the company, which was a far cry from being the boss's brother who had to prove he'd earned each and every promotion and wasn't just being given a free ride out of nepotism.

"Anyway, you make Duncan nervous," Libby said. "He's very nice, and quite competent as long as you aren't around."

"Kane needs someone who's competent no matter what."

She waved her hand, unperturbed. "Duncan will be. I'm going to tell him something outrageous that will make him smile, instead of spill or break something when he sees you."

Neil's self-protective instincts went on full alert. "You don't know anything outrageous about me."

"I wouldn't be so sure of that."

He was sure.

Well, pretty sure.

Kane wouldn't have told Libby about his occasional boyhood exploits, or about the time he'd gone skinny-dipping with a cheerleader in the Puget Sound. Skinny-dipping during a Washington winter wasn't the brightest thing, but neither were teenage jocks. And he couldn't think of anything else she might have heard about in the last eleven years that would qualify as outrageous.

"You don't have anything to tell Dunk about me, unless you make something up," he said severely.

"What a great idea. Thanks. I'll think of something really good."

"Don't you dare," he warned.

"Why not? It was your idea."

His idea?

Right. As if Libby hadn't already thought of inventing some extravagant, ridiculous tale to entertain

Dunk Anderson. Nothing licentious, of course, just embarrassing as hell.

"I don't know what Dunk is doing with the company, anyway," Neil said, trying to change the subject. "Didn't I hear he has a stockbroker's license?"

She dumped handfuls of coffee-soaked tissue into the waste can. "Yes, but he didn't like it. I think you're prejudiced because he's a man, and you think secretaries and assistants should be dutiful, coffee-fetching women, while men should be the power-brokers who run the universe."

"That isn't true. And didn't we have this discussion a few hours ago? I don't have hang-ups about women in business."

She just lifted an eyebrow.

Neil opened his mouth, then closed it again. He might as well forget it. After countless debates with his sisters, he knew women understood a certain logic, men understood another, and there was no meeting in the middle. Particularly with a woman in Libby's mood.

It was his own fault, both for the things he'd said earlier in the day, and for asking her out all those years ago. Some mistakes haunted you forever.

Of course, no one had ever tempted him like Libby Dumont. New on the job, Libby had been assigned to reorganize archived files in a basement of the company's first building...a grim place everyone called the crypt. He'd gotten frustrated waiting for data on an old merger and gone down to get the file himself.

Then he'd seen Libby.

She was reaching up, pushing a teetering box back on a high shelf. Her sweater had pulled tight, defining her body and instantly setting him on fire. She'd glanced in his direction, lost her battle with the box, and was showered with dusty files. Instead of getting angry or embarrassed, she just laughed, her green eyes sparkling like jewels and her long hair falling down her back in a silken torrent of brown and gold and red.

God, he'd loved that laugh.

Unselfconscious, charming, convincing him she was a whole lot more experienced than was really the case.

Neil hesitated, then ran a finger into his collar and tugged on his tie. "By the way, my mother called and suggested I bring you to my nieces' birthday party."

Libby's mouth dropped open.

A children's party?

Wasn't that too prosaic and normal for Neil? Over the years she'd heard Kane talk endlessly about the family; he was devoted to them. Neil seemed fond of his siblings, too, but she'd never imagined him attending a birthday celebration for two four-year-old girls.

"Thanks, but I've got work to do." She would have enjoyed the party and visiting with the rest of the O'Rourke family, but going anywhere with Neil wasn't the best idea—even though she wanted to kick him for looking so relieved at her refusal.

"I'm sure you've already put in enough hours."

"Actually, I have…plans. For the evening." It wasn't a lie. She *did* have plans—laundry, vacuuming, and dosing the cat for fleas. Lately it felt like too much effort going on dates that never seemed to lead anywhere.

"All right. By the way, thanks for the report," he

said, holding up a sheaf of papers. "I'll go over it this weekend, then we'll talk again Monday."

It wasn't until after he'd left that Libby let out the breath she'd been holding.

She could always ask Kane to forget her promotion. He might even be relieved he didn't have to find a new administrative officer. She'd only had the position for a short while, so it wasn't like she was bored with her work or anything.

No.

Her chin lifted stubbornly.

She wouldn't let Neil O'Rourke have the satisfaction of thinking he'd driven her away. And she'd make a darned good vice president, no matter what he might think.

Chapter Three

Neil sat back on the sofa in his mother's living room and listened to the high-pitched squeals of his nieces as they unwrapped their birthday presents.

Damn, they were cute.

They'd also be spoiled right down to their finger-tips if his little sister didn't have so much sense when it came to raising her babies—as his mother's only grandchildren, they were the recipients of all her grandmotherly attention.

Well, they were the only grandchildren until Kane and Beth's baby arrived.

His oldest brother stood in the arched entry of the living room, his arm wrapped possessively around his wife's waist. Occasionally he'd stroke the small swell of her stomach and Beth would look up with a soft warmth in her eyes that excluded everyone else on the planet.

Maddie and Patrick, the latest newlyweds in the family, weren't much better, though at the moment

Maddie was on her knees next to the birthday girls, laughing as they decorated her hair and shoulders with bright ribbons. Little Peggy and Amy seemed to be having more fun playing with their new aunt than opening packages, but nobody minded.

"At least two of my sons have given me grand daughters-in-law," his mother said, sinking down on the sofa beside him, her Irish brogue stronger than usual. She'd come from Ireland as a young wife and had never lost her native accent. "Beth and Maddie are fine women."

"They're a lot alike," Neil murmured. "Being twins."

"True enough." Pegeen O'Rourke nodded happily. "It's sad they were separated as babes, but I'm glad they've found each other at last."

"But even happier they both married into our family," he added dryly.

Pegeen let out a low, rich chuckle. "Aye. I wish all my children could be as happy as Kane and Patrick." She shot a significant glance in his direction. "Perhaps it's time for you to think of finding a wife."

He lifted an eyebrow. "Aren't two sons in the last four months enough? If we all get married, what will you have to look forward to?"

His mother's smile reminded him of a contented cat with cream on its whiskers. "Grandchildren," she said happily.

Lord. He'd set himself up for that one.

"You know how I feel about marriage. Besides, I just got the presidency of a division in the company, and that's much more fun than changing diapers."

She patted his hand. "You never know until you try. The company isn't a great comfort at night."

Neil shook his head.

A long time ago he'd come to the conclusion you couldn't have it all. He didn't even *want* to have it all. He was too single-minded, too selfish. The one time he'd slipped and fallen in love he'd practically flunked out of college, his focus shot to hell. Then she'd turned out to be more interested in using him to make her rich boyfriend jealous, than marrying a guy still in school.

His mouth tightened momentarily, remembering that long ago humiliation, the incredulous voice saying she might marry someone like his brother, but not someone poor, with no money of his own. It just confirmed what he'd suspected all along; marriage wasn't for him.

Especially to a woman like Libby Dumont.

She had a body that wouldn't quit and a Puritan's soul. Being married to a woman like that would drive a man insane. Why, Libby was probably still a virgin. Of course, there was nothing wrong with being a virgin, all girls started out that way. But making love to her would be like making love to a block of ice.

Wouldn't it?

An image of how she had looked that afternoon— eyes flashing and angry color flooding her cheeks— went flying through his mind. She was obviously more passionate than he'd always believed.

Not that he wanted Libby as a lover.

Yet Neil shifted uncomfortably, remembering how his body had come to attention from a simple contact with her leg. It was hard to shut the door on old feelings, and she represented the last time he'd lost control—a vestige of high school days, of necking in cars and hoping to get lucky. He'd acted badly, then tried to put the blame on her like an immature kid. Not that it changed anything now; apologies so long after the fact were meaningless.

But Libby was right about one thing, they didn't get along for a number of reasons, most of them having nothing to do with the past.

"I do wish Libby could have come tonight," said his mother.

For an instant Neil wondered if she'd guessed he was thinking about Libby—something he was doing far too much—then decided he was being paranoid.

"She said she was busy."

Across the room Dylan stood talking with Connor, the youngest of the O'Rourke sons, and Pegeen looked at him unhappily. "Do you think someone is courting Libby, and that's why she couldn't come tonight? Oh, if only Dylan had asked her out at Kane and Beth's wedding when they were getting on so well," she said, sounding thoroughly exasperated.

His nerves tightened. "Libby isn't thinking about getting married, if that's what you're worried about."

"And how would you be knowin' that?"

Damnation. Why had he opened his mouth? Now his mom would think there was something going on between him and Libby. "We were talking, that's all, and she mentioned it."

"Seems an odd thing to just say."

Neil tugged at the neck of his shirt. He'd removed his tie earlier, but it felt tight, nonetheless. "It isn't odd. I had to find out what her future plans were since she's going to be my vice president."

"What difference would that make?" Pegeen's question sounded like something Libby would say.

"It's just…uh, in her new position she's going to

be busy, have a lot to do, and getting married, that would be very distract..." His mother's wise eyes were crinkled with amusement at his discomfort, so Neil gave up and slumped against the cushions. "Never mind," he muttered.

Normally he enjoyed family gatherings, but tonight was an exception. It was little wonder, between his matchmaking mom and the edgy tension gripping him.

He was restless.

Charged up.

Ready to dive into running his division of the company and getting things set up the way he wanted them. He couldn't afford to be distracted, and Libby was turning into one hell of a distraction.

Even when she wasn't anywhere around.

By the time Neil reached work on Monday he was convinced he'd gotten everything out of his system. All the questions and confusion and mixed feelings. And the temptation.

He and Libby weren't lover material.

Any interest in changing that condition probably stemmed from his ego. Basically, he was a man who thrived on challenges, and Libby was a challenge from the word go. Working with her would be another challenge, but he could do it. The best plan was to get the project off and running so they could focus on other duties that didn't involve such close contact.

Stopping in front of Libby's office, Neil watched for a moment unobserved.

She was outside in the secretary's cubicle, Dunk's gaze glued to her as she explained something. Dunk was a tall towhead, with hands and limbs that seemed too big for the rest of him. Though Neil expected to see something break or fly apart at any minute, nothing happened. Dunk even managed to safely pour himself a cup of coffee.

It was only when he turned around that he got nervous, and only when he spotted Neil.

"Mr. O'Rourke, h-hello."

Mr. O'Rourke?

Libby was right, that did sound stuffy.

"Hi, Duncan. Please call me Neil."

Dunk's face was dubious. "Yes, sir. Thank you. I will…yes." He edged away and hurried down the corridor.

Sir?

Great, that was certainly an improvement.

Neil looked at Libby in time to see her wipe a smile from her lips. "Good morning," she said cheerfully.

At least she hadn't called him Mr. O'Rourke, as well.

"Good morning. Did you enjoy your plans on Friday?"

She looked at him blankly. "Plans?"

"The reason you couldn't attend my nieces' birthday party."

"Oh, fine." Libby thought about her quiet Friday evening. She'd spent it scribbling down notes for the bed-and-breakfast proposal. Real exciting stuff. The biggest adrenaline rush of the entire weekend was when she'd dreamed something utterly inappropriate about Neil, but she couldn't mention *that.* "How is your mother and Dylan and everyone?"

"Dylan?"

Libby frowned at the odd look on Neil's face. Honestly, he got stranger by the hour. "Yes, Dylan and the rest of the family."

"They're fine. Mother said you and Dylan visited for a long time at Kane and Beth's wedding reception."

Her frown deepened. She *had* talked with Dylan at the reception, though hardly for hours and hours. "He was being friendly since I was there alone and didn't know many of the guests," she said finally.

"Is that all?"

All?

"Your brother is very nice," she said, bewildered by Neil's intense expression.

With any another man Libby might have guessed he was jealous, but Neil wasn't the jealous type, and there was nothing going on between them, anyway. Well…not much. He'd announced he was still attracted to her, supposedly as a way to get everything out in the open. As if *that* meant anything.

"Kane's nice. Dylan is nice. But you never said what I was," he mused.

Oh, right.

Like she was going to hang herself on a few choice words. Neil was the brother of the CEO, and clearing the air didn't mean she could say whatever she wanted. Yet a tantalizing thought occurred to Libby, namely that a second kiss might clear the air better than words. After all, they could get any lingering attraction out of their system that way and second kisses were often complete duds. Her not-so-inspiring love life largely consisted of dull kisses and boring evenings with men consumed by their stock portfolios.

"Libby?"

She blinked and drew a steadying breath.

Some ideas were dumber than others, and kissing Neil again was the dumbest of them all. She was better off with her boring evenings.

"I…uh, I've done more research and compiled a list of properties throughout Washington and Oregon that we could consider for acquisition."

"Changing the subject?"

"It seems like a good idea," she said through gritted teeth, holding out the neatly bound material she'd assembled.

"You must have worked over the weekend." He sounded surprised, which made her want to kick him…a common impulse when it came to Neil. There was nothing remarkable about her working Saturdays, though she usually spent Sundays in Endicott with her parents, helping out.

"Yes," she said shortly.

She tried not to watch as he flipped through the report, but it was difficult when she didn't have anything else to do.

Lord, he was nice to look at.

He wore a designer suit, the kind she saw on models, but no model had ever looked that good. His shoulders were broad and his stomach flat, with tapered hips and long straight legs. It was so irritating. Neil had looks, intelligence, talent, a Harvard education, a great family, and still managed to be the most impossible man ever born.

"I'm impressed," he said after a moment, his brow creased. And even *that* was gorgeous on him; most people just looked cross when they frowned. "It's very comprehensive. We'll be able to work off this when we go out scouting."

"You still plan to do the scouting yourself, then?"

His eyebrows shot upward. "I'm planning for *us* to do it, yes. You're the one who said my approach lacked the personal touch Kane wanted for the project." There was a slight edge in his voice—Neil O'Rourke wasn't accustomed to criticism.

Libby tried not to look intimidated.

Or apologize.

"I appreciate the work you've done," he said, gesturing with the hand that held the report. "The sooner we get the ball moving, the sooner we can move on to other projects."

She opened her mouth, then closed it, deciding she shouldn't say anything. Once the bed-and-breakfast line was running, the whole project would most likely be moved to another division. If Neil knew she wanted to stay involved, he'd probably say something sarcastic.

He dropped the report in his briefcase. "Has Kane mentioned moving into your new office?"

She blinked. "My new office?"

"You've been assigned the executive suite next to mine. Temporarily, at least, until everything is decided on the reorganization."

"Oh."

Wasn't that terrific?

Next door. Right at Neil O'Rourke's beck and call.

"I'll send someone up to pack up your things."

Was he offering because he didn't think she was capable, or because...Libby sighed and shook her head. She couldn't keep assuming the worst about him. He *had* tried to be nice to Duncan Anderson, which was a lot more than he'd ever done before, and he was asking her opinion on things she'd never expected to have a say about.

"I can manage."

"Good. I'd like to present Kane with a strategy on the bed-and-breakfast inn project within a few days, and we should also develop a plan on establishing the new division to give him."

She cocked her head. "You mean you don't have everything decided and mapped out already? What's wrong, weren't you feeling well? You had the entire weekend."

Contrary to what she expected, Neil grinned. "I would have, but Kane wants us to practice team management."

He sauntered out, looking his usual confident self, but it didn't annoy Libby as much as usual. It was hard to imagine them ever becoming friends, but she supposed that sooner or later they would end up getting along…or killing each other.

She spent the next hour packing her personal belongings and overseeing the transfer to her new suite. When she arrived at Neil's office he was talking to Margie Clarke, who looked positively desperate as she took notes between answering the phone and nodding her head at his rapid-fire instructions. Libby gave her a sympathetic smile.

"Maybe you could give her a crash course in multitasking," Neil muttered as he closed the door behind them.

"Maybe you could lighten up and give her a chance to settle in." Libby wanted to tell him about Margie's sick daughter, but hesitated. If Margie wanted Neil to know, she would have said something to him about it herself.

He dropped onto his couch. "And maybe you were right about Tam Tam the Barracuda being right for the job. She's really very good. I'm considering bringing her back."

"You…are?"

A stab of jealousy caught Libby by surprise.

Tami Berkut was nice enough—a little confused about what she wanted out of life, but she wasn't the only one. Libby knew she wanted something more herself; she just didn't know how to get it.

"Mrs. Clarke isn't working out as well as I'd hoped," Neil said, tapping his fingers on his desk.

"Margie just needs some time."

"Perhaps." He leaned forward, fixing her with one of his amused, all-knowing looks. "In the meantime we need to start looking for our first bed-and-breakfast inn. I've taken a look at your list, and found three prospects in a little town called Endicott. Ever hear of it?"

Libby fought to control the familiar warmth in her face. Okay, so she'd decided to include Endicott on the list. Was it fair to ignore a favorable location just because it was her hometown?

"Of course I've heard of it."

"Yes. According to your personnel records, your parents live there."

"I grew up in Endicott," Libby said, an edge to her voice. "It used to be a prosperous vacation town in both summer and winter, but that was a long time ago. Wealthy Seattle families used to build summer places in the area."

His smile was infuriating. Knowing Neil, he'd already checked the whole thing out and was just yanking her chain for the fun of it.

"Why were you reading my personnel records?" she added.

For the first time that she could remember, he looked uncomfortable. "Curiosity."

Yeah, curious how he could annoy her even more.

Maybe he was hoping she'd get tired of it, or be scared off, or otherwise ask Kane to change his mind. Well, too bad. He'd have to learn that country girl or not, she didn't scare so easily.

"I realize Endicott is a little rural for your tastes," she said edgily. "But there are a number of properties close to the Interstate corridor that might interest you."

"I didn't say I wasn't interested. It sounds like a nice enough place, and since you have contacts in the town, we might as well start there. Are you ready to go?"

Her jaw dropped.

He sounded serious.

"You want to drive up there today?"

"You think I can't find the way without a trail of breadcrumbs? You'll be along as a guide, so we won't get lost in the wilds of Washington."

"Yes. I mean, no. That is, it's not hard to find. You just head toward Mount Rainier."

Neil grinned at the nonplussed look on Libby's face. He loved how flustered she got, though apparently it was mostly with him because people were always talking about how calm and unflappable she was in a crisis.

"It's a long drive."

"Not that long, we can be there well before noon. We won't have to stay overnight, though eventually we'll need to on some of our scouting trips."

"Overnight?"

"Yes. Business trips can go overnight." Neil shifted uncomfortably, trying to resist the urge to explain himself. Could Libby be so innocent she was reading something inappropriate into the idea of them traveling together? It wasn't as if he'd suggested they share a room. Yet even as he wondered, he realized his voice had dropped to a husky murmur when he said "overnight."

Damn.

He'd never had so much trouble with a female colleague. But then, none of them had been Libby Dumont. There was a feeling of unfinished business between them that made things awkward. Of course, Libby would say it was the male perspective making him think that way, but he wasn't so certain. On some level she was aware of him as a man, whether she was willing to admit it or not.

"Are you afraid to be alone with me in a car?" he asked. "Maybe you're thinking about the last time we went somewhere together and—"

"That's ridiculous." Libby slapped her pad of paper down on the corner of a table and stood up. "I'll get my things and be right back."

"All right, I'll call the real estate office to be sure they can show us the properties today."

Neil hid a smile as she hurried off; he wasn't the only one who responded to a challenge. Yet his amusement faded as he remembered questioning her about Dylan. His brother *had* enjoyed Libby's company, he'd even asked about her a couple times since Kane's wedding.

But what bothered Neil for some reason was the idea that Libby had liked Dylan.

Chapter Four

Libby's pulse pounded as she hurried past Margie Clarke's desk. She suspected Neil was trying to manipulate her, but couldn't accuse him of it without starting another argument.

He was rotten.

Maybe she *wasn't* cut out for big business. How could you survive so much stress? Of course, her stress mostly came from the man she was supposed to be working with.

She walked inside her new office and took several deep, calming breaths. It was a calm place—twice as big as her old one, with long windows that framed views of the Puget Sound and modern, expensive furniture. O'Rourke Enterprises always bought quality.

You're going up in the world, Libby thought.

But it wasn't what she'd always wanted, more like a pale substitute. All her hometown friends were married, even the ones who'd sworn they'd never get "tied down" like that. A dozen kids in Endicott called her Aunt Libby, but it wasn't the same as being a wife and mother.

"What's wrong with me?" she whispered, rubbing her temples.

She had a good life, except when she was worried about her mother. Pneumonia had weakened Faye Dumont's heart when Libby was sixteen, and since then Libby had spent her share of sleepless nights whenever Faye had a "spell." But all people had worries of some kind.

"Are you okay?"

The question made Libby jump. She whirled and saw Neil standing in the doorway.

"Er...yes."

"You were rubbing your forehead. Headache?"

She had a headache all right—Neil O'Rourke. He was the worst kind of headache.

"I didn't sleep well last night, that's all." Libby picked up her purse from the desk.

"Allow me," he murmured, taking her coat and holding it up.

Swallowing, Libby slid her arms into the jacket and tried to ignore how warm his hands felt on her shoulders. She turned abruptly, her eyes level with the knot in his tie, scant inches away. Slowly she tipped her head back and stared into Neil's face. They hadn't been this close to each other since that long ago night, and the same old butterflies began dancing in her midriff.

And the same old doubts.

How many times had she wished they'd met later, when she was more certain of herself? How many times had she told herself it didn't matter, she didn't like him anyway? She believed in commitment, while the only thing he was committed to was making a profit.

Neil O'Rourke was the most sophisticated man she'd ever known. Even if he wasn't a prince, around him she felt like Cinderella *before* the fairy god-mother showed up. And who ever believed the prince fell in love with Cinderella in the first place? Beneath her magical ball gown Cinderella was still a country bumpkin, and he was a prince.

His fingers brushed her cheek and Libby shivered in response. The expression in his face was intense, unreadable, and a deep ache went through her body. It was so inappropriate, he was the last man she should respond to like that.

"Neil?" she whispered.

"I'm not the big bad wolf," he murmured. "You don't have to look at me like I'm going to eat you."

"That's not what I was thinking."

"What, then?"

Libby's gaze dropped to the sensual curve of his lips before she could help herself. What would he think if he knew how often she thought about his mouth and the way he'd once… She put a brake on her unruly brain.

"Nothing."

"Are you sure?" The husky question made her swallow.

The last time she'd heard Neil sound like that was eleven years ago, right before he'd started kissing her.

"Are we going, or aren't we?" she asked, hoping the way her breasts had tightened wouldn't be too obvious.

"We're going."

They made their way down to the underground

parking garage, but when they stopped in front of a silver Chevy Blazer, she gazed at it in surprise.

"This is yours?"

"Yeah, what did you expect?" Neil asked, inexplicably annoyed. It was just a car and he didn't know why Libby's opinion mattered, yet he still found himself tensing as he waited for an answer.

"I don't know. A Jaguar, maybe. Or a Volvo," she offered tentatively.

Laughter rose in Neil's chest. "There's a world of difference between a Jag and a Volvo. What kind of ideas about me do you have running around in your mind?"

Her eyelids dropped and she lifted her shoulders. "I'm sure you wouldn't be interested."

That's what you think, he said silently as Libby climbed inside the Blazer. No matter what he told himself, he was too damned interested in her. She had to pull her skirt up a few inches to negotiate the high step and his temperature hiked several notches at the sight of sleek, silky skin. She had such a nice body it was easy to overlook her killer legs.

After they pulled onto the freeway he cast a glance at Libby and saw her face was turned, looking out the side window. He flexed his fingers on the steering wheel, debating what to say. But the miles ticked by in silence until he realized she had fallen asleep.

A curious warmth unfurled inside his chest.

She disliked him, but apparently she trusted him that much.

The clean scent of pine and cedar drew Libby back to awareness—it was the smell of home. She straightened in her seat, groaning at the realization she'd fallen asleep.

"Uh…" Words failed her.

"You've been very quiet. I hope I haven't bored you," Neil said.

Quiet? Libby tried to figure out if she was relieved or insulted he hadn't noticed her snoozing, then decided it was a mixture of both. No matter what her feelings were about Neil, a woman liked to think she was…well, *noticeable*.

"My cell phone is in my suit pocket. Why don't you give the real estate office a call and let them know we'll be there soon?" He reached into the rear seat of the Blazer and handed her the coat.

For some reason delving into Neil's pockets seemed an intimate thing to do, but she could imagine how he'd react if she said so. Swallowing, she cautiously fished out the phone and dialed the number.

"Hello, Ginger? It's Libby Dumont."

"Hey, Libby, I guess you're on the way. I talked to Mr. O'Rourke earlier. I'm so thrilled about the bed-and-breakfast idea. It could save Endicott," Ginger said fervently. She was a close friend and they'd talked about the project at church that Sunday.

Libby cast a quick glance at Neil. "Yes, I know. We just wanted to let you know we'll be there soon."

"You sound uptight. Mr. Steamroller must be listening."

"Er…yes."

Ginger chuckled. She was a bubbly redhead with three kids and a husband who thought the sun rose and set in her. Libby had told her something about Neil, so she knew about his tendency to mow down everything in his path on his way to success.

"Do your folks know you'll be in town? Somebody's bound to mention you were here."

Libby winced.

She'd meant to phone her parents, if only to explain why she couldn't see them, but there hadn't been time. "No. We're going to be tied up viewing the properties."

"I'll give them a call. I don't suppose the bossman wants to drop around for a family visit."

"That's definitely not on the agenda."

Ginger made a disgusted sound. "That guy must be a real piece of work."

"You have no idea." The words came out more fervently than Libby had intended, and she was glad Neil couldn't hear both sides of the conversation.

"I'm glad I'm not in your shoes. We'll see you in a bit."

She disconnected the call and slid the cell phone back into his coat pocket. "Mrs. Ellender is expecting us."

"Good."

Libby figured Ginger would make a good impression on Neil—she was stacked like a Miss America and knew her stuff as a real estate agent. Two things he was bound to appreciate. But when they walked into the office, her friend rushed out of the back room, looking harried.

"I'm so sorry, but I've got to go," she said. "The school just called to say my oldest hurt his arm."

"Harry?" Libby asked. Harry was her godson and even if he was a fearless daredevil who never seemed to get seriously injured, she couldn't help worrying.

"I'm sure another agent can show us the properties we're interested in," Neil interrupted smoothly. "If we make an offer we'll work out something with the commission so you get a percentage.''

Neil saw Libby and the buxom redhead exchange glances.

''Uh...Endicott only has *one* real estate agent,'' Mrs. Ellender said. ''And that's me.''

He groaned silently, wondering how they would ever get the project going if they had to deal with towns so small they didn't have adequate services.

''But I'll just give you the keys and Libby can take you around,'' the redhead added. ''I'll be back in the office later, and we can talk then.''

He stared, nonplussed. ''I'm sure your clients wouldn't like that.''

Mrs. Ellender waved her hand in a pooh poohing motion. ''Don't worry about it. The properties were deeded to Endicott years ago, so the town is my client, so to speak.''

''But surely the community would prefer an authorized representative to go with us.''

''It's okay. Libby is our pastor's daughter. If we can't trust her, we can't trust anyone.'' She handed Libby three sets of keys. ''It's probably just a sprain, but they're going to X-ray the arm to make sure,'' she said in an undertone. ''I'll see you later.''

After she'd rushed away, driving a sturdy truck with an extended cab, Neil looked at Libby in astonishment.

''This can't be okay with the authorities.''

Libby shrugged, not looking particularly surprised. ''Ginger's husband is the mayor and sheriff and fire chief, so nobody's going to object.''

''But in the city—''

''This isn't the city,'' she said. ''Don't you know

anything about small towns? Little places where everyone volunteers because there isn't a budget for the extras like a paid fire chief. Or firemen.''

''You don't have a fire department?''

''I didn't say that.''

She pointed down the street and he saw the Endicott Volunteer Fire Department, sitting on the corner. It was a quaint vintage building that looked barely big enough for an old horse and ladder truck.

Holy cow.

It was like landing on a different planet where all the rules were different.

''Shall we go see one of the houses, or get something to eat first?'' Libby asked. ''We only have a café and pizza parlor in Endicott, but they're both good. Ginger runs the pizza parlor, too.''

Bemusedly, Neil noticed the real estate agency and pizza joint all seemed to be part of the same business. ''Uh…we can eat later. Let's see some of the property you thought would work for the project.''

Maybe that way he could shake his feeling of being a fish out of water.

Though Libby was concerned about her godson, she couldn't help marveling at the sight of a baffled Neil O'Rourke. He was always so suave and sophisticated, so sure of himself in any situation. It was almost endearing to see him gawking at Endicott's only traffic light and the old fashioned gas street lamps the city had converted to electric, rather than replace them.

''How did these places get deeded to the town?'' he asked as they pulled up to the first house.

"Partly out of civic pride, and partly because they became too much trouble," Libby admitted.

Huckleberry House stood a little way outside of town, a frosted cake sort of home built during the heyday of Edwardian architecture. She'd never been inside because it was owned by a New Yorker who'd inherited the property from a distant cousin. A year before he'd decided to donate it to Endicott rather than keep paying taxes on a house he couldn't find a buyer for, and didn't want to live in.

"Looks pretty run-down," Neil said.

"Ginger says the underlying structure is sound."

"What do you expect her to say?" he asked impatiently. "She's a real estate agent and wants a commission."

Libby glared. "You're impossible. She would never lie to me—I'm her son's godmother, for heaven's sake."

"Libby, you can't believe—"

"Get back in the car if you feel that way," she snapped. "I've wanted to see this house my entire life and you aren't going to spoil it."

Neil whistled beneath his breath. He didn't have any intention of just sitting in the Blazer while Libby risked life and limb in a dump that should have been condemned decades ago. "I didn't say I wasn't interested in seeing it."

"Fine." Libby fumbled with the keys she'd been given until she found the one that fit the lock.

His eyes widened slightly when he realized it was an old skeleton key. They walked inside and Neil held his breath. Yet as decrepit as the porch had seemed, the interior hardwood floor seemed sturdy.

"It's incredible," Libby whispered, gazing raptly around.

He looked as well, but all he saw were grimy sheets thrown over furniture and windows that barely admitted light because they were so dirty. A thick layer of dust covered everything and cobwebs shrouded the corners with a macabre lacy art.

"Once upon a time they threw elegant parties in Huckleberry House," Libby murmured. "The chandelier would have sparkled in the gas light, and men in high pointed collars escorted ladies in dresses that swept the floor. Everything would have gleamed from being polished and waxed. It should look that way again."

A peculiar sensation swept through Neil. Libby *wasn't* seeing the dirt and grime, she saw the possibilities beneath it, the old glories of a house that must have been a showplace in its day.

She saw potential.

And she would have fit right into the gracious Edwardian society that had built Huckleberry House, from her strawberry and cream complexion, to the long, luxuriant hair that hung down her back. It was easy to imagine her in a long, graceful dress, her hair piled softly on her head and set with jeweled combs.

All at once Libby blinked and looked at him.

"I suppose you hate it," she said.

Hate it?

How could he hate a place described like that? Neil tried to tell himself he was being influenced by his visceral reaction to a beautiful woman, rather than sound business sense, but it didn't seem to matter.

"I think it's great," he said slowly.

A radiant smile lit her face. "Really?"

"Really. Huckleberry House is going to be our first historic bed-and-breakfast inn. The flagship of the line. Even the name is perfect."

"I knew it." She threw her arms around him for a second, then gasped and stepped backward. "S-sorry."

Neil, who prided himself on his control, felt it slipping away. "Don't apologize," he said, pulling her back.

Libby gulped as she stared into Neil's gray eyes, her body pressed full length to his. He didn't look cool at the moment, far from it, yet after a long minute he shuddered and dropped his arms.

"I shouldn't have done that," he muttered.

"I'm not so sure," Libby whispered. Life was full of shouldn'ts and uncertainty, something she'd learned when her mother got sick. "I've been thinking about things," she breathed, daring to touch a crisp lock of hair on Neil's forehead.

"Yeah?" He sounded hoarse. "About what things?"

"About what you said…that we should clear the air."

His forehead wrinkled in confusion. "You want to *talk?*" It didn't sound as if he was interested in a discussion, which seemed like a good sign since she didn't really want to talk, either.

"No. There might be another way."

"How?"

"We could try kissing again."

She would never have had the nerve to suggest it if he hadn't hugged her back, but he had, and she really wanted be kissed by the only man who'd ever made all the nerves in her body stand at attention.

"*That's* going to clear the air?"

"It seems to me we could get this attraction thing sorted out that way. I mean, we don't really like each other, so it ought to go away easily enough."

Neil would have laughed, but he knew Libby wouldn't understand. God, she was so innocent. Did she really think attraction would dissipate through a kiss, like electricity through a lightning rod? And did she realize she'd just admitted she was attracted to him? Probably not, and he certainly wasn't going to point it out to her—his mama and daddy hadn't raised a fool.

"I'm willing to try if you are," he said, ignoring every single instinct for good sense that he possessed.

"I'm the one who suggested it."

He inhaled the scent of vanilla and his gut twisted. Kissing her was a really dumb idea, but he was still going to do it—eleven years of declaring he shouldn't get involved with someone from work wasn't enough to stop him. But he'd barely had a chance to brush his lips across hers when he heard a car drive up.

"No," he groaned.

Libby jerked away and put a hand to her throat. What had she nearly done? And to make things worse, she still wanted to do it.

"Sweetheart?" called her father.

She winced.

They'd left the door wide-open, so he could have easily seen them, along with anyone else who'd come along. The story would have flown around Endicott at light speed. She'd grown up here and the people expected her to behave a certain way as the preacher's daughter. She didn't mind, but sometimes she wanted to feel free as anyone else to make mistakes and get on with her life.

"Dad?" She hurried out to the rickety porch. "Is everything all right?"

"Fine, dear. Ginger mentioned you were visiting properties with your boss, so your mother thought you might be able to come for lunch."

"I'm Neil O'Rourke." Neil said from behind her. "Good to meet you."

"Timothy Dumont. You will come to lunch, won't you?"

"We'd love to. *Reverend* Dumont, isn't it?"

Her father gave Neil a genial smile. "That's right, but call me Timothy, like everyone else."

He turned, obviously expecting them to follow, and Libby wanted to drop out of sight. She adored her dad, but Neil wasn't a down-home sort of guy.

"We don't have to go," she said when they got into the Blazer. "I'll call my mother and make an excuse."

Neil reversed, then swung out to follow Reverend Dumont's Dodge pickup. It seemed as if everyone in Endicott owned a truck, he mused, but it was probably a practical choice when you lived on the side of a mountain.

"I wouldn't have said yes if I hadn't meant it," he said, glancing at Libby.

Of course, he'd much rather be kissing her, but since that activity seemed to be temporarily put on hold, eating lunch was probably the best alternative.

Well, he hoped it was temporary.

The more he thought about it, the more he thought

she was right. They might be able to clear the air with a good kiss.

His conscience let out a sarcastic laugh, but he decided to ignore it along with the rest of his good sense.

Chapter Five

Timothy Dumont stopped in front of a small white house next to a church, and Neil pulled in behind him. A tidy white picket fence confined the front lawn, but the backyard was an unfenced natural meadow. In his mind's eye he could see Libby as a carefree child, spinning happily, with the mountain as her playground.

It was a curiously endearing image, sweet and uncomplicated, though there was nothing uncomplicated about the woman she'd become.

The door of the house opened and an older version of Libby appeared. Libby waved and climbed out. "Hi, Mom," she called.

"Hello, darling."

Neil put his palm on the small of Libby's back and she jumped. "Aren't you going to introduce me?" he asked softly.

"Mom, this is Neil O'Rourke," she said dutifully,

though the tension in her shoulders announced she wasn't happy. "This is my mother, Faye Dumont."

"It's lovely to meet you, Neil. I hope you're enjoying your visit to Endicott." Faye put out her hand to shake and Neil took an instant liking to her. Of course, he doubted either of the Dumonts would be so cordial if they knew about his licentious thoughts over their daughter.

"I'm enjoying it very much," he said. "We're thinking about buying Huckleberry House as the first in a line of bed-and-breakfast inns. It seems logical to start in a town that one of us knows well. Besides, I've been curious to see where Libby grew up."

Libby made a choking sound behind him, but he ignored her. It was true, he *had* been curious what sort of place had produced a woman of such striking contradictions.

"Are you all right, dear?" Faye asked, patting her daughter's arm.

"I'm fine." Libby's glare from under the thick fringe of her lashes should have fried him on the spot.

"Good. Do come in, Neil. We love visitors, especially when they bring our daughter along."

As they followed, he leaned close to Libby and whispered in her ear. "At least one Dumont calls me Neil. This is going well, don't you think?"

"I think you're a shameless liar. Curious to see where I grew up? Give me a break."

"I'm employing diplomacy—your parents are leaders in the community. We need them on our side to build support for the project. We wouldn't want any protest marches or anything to get in the way of our development."

"Protest marches over a bed-and-breakfast inn that will bring good decent business into town?"

"It could happen."

Libby shook her head pityingly. "You really don't know anything about small towns, do you?"

A half hour later Libby shook her head as she looked at her father sitting with Neil at the kitchen table. The two men were talking about fishing, which wasn't surprising since it was one of her dad's passions—he could spent hours in a cold trout stream, communing with nature and angling for the silvered rainbow fish. But it was Neil's interest in the subject that was so surprising.

"He's a nice man," said her mother. They were cleaning salad greens to go along with lunch.

"Ah-huh," Libby murmured.

"You've never said anything about Neil. You talk about Kane, but not his brother."

Libby wiped her fingers on a dish towel. "That's because he just recently came into the picture."

Liar screamed her conscience, though she hadn't really lied. They were talking about who she worked for, and working with Neil *was* new, except for his brief tenure as CEO. But if she'd described Neil and his slash and burn business style, they would have said it wasn't charitable to say so, and that maybe he just needed some understanding.

Her parents thought everyone had a heart of gold, even when it was buried under a ton of tarnish.

Faye winked mischievously. "He's very attractive, dear, and he watches you when he doesn't think you'll notice."

"Really." Libby resisted rolling her eyes.

Neil O'Rourke was one of the most eligible—and dedicated—bachelors in Seattle. If he was watching her it was to figure out how to best to tease her about being a preacher's daughter. Faye Dumont was just giving into a weakness some mothers were guilty of—thinking their daughters were irresistible.

"Are you seeing anyone, dear? Someone special?" Faye asked, her voice more normal now that she wasn't asking questions about their unexpected lunch guest.

Libby pulled a bottle of balsamic vinegar from the cupboard, stalling for a moment. Her parents' questions about dating were becoming more frequent and urgent, they must be getting anxious for grandchildren.

"Darling?"

"I've been really busy, Mom, working extra hours and settling into my new house. Everything else is taking a back seat for a while."

"You don't have to spend so much time up here in Endicott," Faye said slowly. "We love seeing you, but you should think more about your own life."

Libby grimaced, hoping Neil couldn't hear their conversation, or at least that he wasn't interested enough to listen; he'd be convinced she lived like a cloistered nun when it came to men. His opinion—right or wrong—shouldn't bother her, but the feminine ego wasn't particularly intelligent.

"I like coming up on the weekends."

"Yes, darling, but I'm much better now and you ought to spend more time with your friends."

"Uh…okay. The salad is ready," Libby announced, hastily tossing the greens with the seasoned dressing. "Are you hungry? Everything is ready."

"I still say I should have taken you all out to lunch," Neil said, taking the bowl and carrying it to the dining room.

"Mom enjoys cooking for company," Libby said.

"It looked like you did most of it," he murmured.

She cast him a pleading glance, shaking her head minutely. To her relief he didn't say anything more, instead complimenting the patchwork quilt hanging on the living room wall.

Her mother beamed. "Thank you, Neil. That's called the double wedding ring pattern. Libby made it."

Libby groaned. "No, I *helped* the quilting circle make it while I was in high school."

She refused to look at Neil, certain she'd see a smug smile on his handsome face. The quilt would be one more bit of proof that she was out of step with the modern world. Yet even as she formed the thought, she lifted her chin. Patchwork quilts were a beautiful and uniquely American art form. If he couldn't appreciate that, then *he* was the one with a problem.

Thankfully, the following conversation was filled with discussion of the weather and fishing, two subjects which were relatively safe when it came to her name being mentioned. But she was surprised when Neil insisting on helping with the dishes.

"Don't look so shocked," he murmured, skillfully loading the dishwasher she'd gotten her parents a few years before. "The family has Sunday dinner each week with my mother, and we always help cook, then clean the kitchen afterward."

"Don't Shannon and your other sisters do that?"

Neil gave her a look of mock horror. "Shannon?

She's a domestic menace. We don't let her near the kitchen if we can help it.''

"Oh." Libby averted her face. Shannon O'Rourke was an expert public relations director for her brother's company, but she *was* a disaster when it came to things domestic. She'd even been banned from using the microwave in the executives' personal area because she'd started two fires in less than a month.

"Besides," he said, "expecting women to do all the work is out of date, don't you think?"

Libby snapped the lid on a container of leftovers. "I didn't say it was right, just what usually happens. When my extended family gets together, the men think the ten minutes they spend loading the dishwasher is an equal contribution to a meal it took hours to prepare."

"You don't mind that?"

Neil sounded curious, rather than critical, so she peeked in his direction. "Sometimes I'd prefer visiting with relatives I haven't seen in long time," she admitted. "But somebody needs to put a meal on the table, and if we left it to my father and brother and uncles we'd have frozen pizza and Twinkies."

When the last pot was dried and put away, Neil leaned against the counter. He'd long since removed his suit jacket, and now his sleeves were rolled above his elbows. If possible, he looked even more gorgeous.

"We should stay in town for a while to see if that real estate agent gets back to her office—I want to arrange for a structural inspection of the Huckleberry House," he said. "We'll also have to do a market analysis. And we should take another look at the

house, too. We never got past the foyer…if you recall.''

His eyes glinted, reminding her of their near-kiss
in the deserted house—not that it would be repeated,
no matter how much her body favored jumping in
with both feet. It had been an impulse of the moment,
and a harebrained one, at that.

''I take it you're changing your mind about buying
Huckleberry House,'' Libby said as coolly as possible.

''No, but we have to make a sound business decision, rather than one based on sentiment. It's Kane's
money, not ours.''

Ah, *this* was the Neil she knew best.

He might be a maverick risk-taker, but it was only
for the sake of the bottom line.

No sentiment whatsoever.

Libby swallowed a stab of illogical disappointment.

He was right, after all, it *was* Kane O'Rourke's
money. But she wanted to save Huckleberry House
so badly it was frustrating to talk about structural in-
spections and market analyses.

Because it was an unseasonably warm day for mid-
December, Neil suggested they walk to Huckleberry
House so he could get a better ''feel'' for Endicott.

''This is a nice place,'' he murmured as they
passed the small white church. Despite the town's obvious financial struggles, the building was well-
maintained.

''I suppose you consider the city your hometown,''
Libby said. ''While there's no hiding that I'm a small
town girl, is there?'' She tugged at the worn sweatshirt she'd unearthed from a hall closet and tied

around her waist. With the sun shining on her hair she looked completely at ease in the rural setting, while he probably stuck out like a neon sign.

It was a strange feeling. One he didn't like, so he tried to think of something else.

"I just realized we have something in common," he said. "Your parents are pushing you to have a more active social life, and my mother thinks I should get married."

Heat burned in her cheeks. "You shouldn't eavesdrop."

"Hey, I was in the same room. That's not eavesdropping." He shielded his eyes from the sun as he looked down at her. "I think they feel guilty."

Guilty?

She frowned. "Why would they feel guilty?"

"Apparently you've given up a lot to help them."

"That's ridiculous. They're my family. Why should anyone feel guilty?"

Normally he would have kept his mouth shut, but Neil knew a lot about guilt. His brother wanted to shower the family with the fruits of his labor, never realizing they felt guilty about the way he'd worked and sacrificed to take care of them.

And, from what he'd learned from the Dumonts, he knew Libby had done much the same. She'd turned down a prestigious out-of-state scholarship because of her mother's illness, helped put her brother through college, and spent most of her free time in Endicott. Obviously she had qualities he'd never expected.

Special qualities.

Family came first with Libby. She didn't consider her choices to be sacrifices, just the things you do when you loved people. And an uneasy feeling swept through Neil as he realized how much he admired her ability to love wholeheartedly.

She tipped her head back, hair shining in the winter sun, a combination of dark and light shading that shifted with each movement. It was a unique color— a warm brown, yet shot with gold, and burnished red in broad sunlight. Neil stuck his hands in his pockets to resist temptation. Eleven years ago that cool, heavy length had flowed through his fingers like liquid silver, spilling around his wrists and arms. Come to think of it, he'd been partial to long hair ever since.

He cleared his throat. "Your mother started having heart problems when you were a teenager?"

"I was sixteen. She's better now, but she has periods when her heart skips beats or there's arrhythmia. The doctor says she'll eventually need a pacemaker."

"The doctor doesn't think she needs surgery now?"

"We don't know." A subtle tension rippled through her. "Mom stopped seeing the specialist a year ago. She said she was fine—that all he was doing was asking a few questions, listening to her chest with a cold stethoscope, and charging too much money."

Neil hesitated, knowing he was the last person from whom Libby wanted advice. "I guess all you can do is try not to worry so much."

"Yeah, that's going to happen." Her voice was a mixture of wry humor and sarcasm.

He sighed. "All right, but you could reduce the number of hours you spend at the company. No one should give up having a life for their work."

"Oh?" Libby's eyebrows rose. "Since when did you decide that?"

"Hey, I bugged Kane for years to get himself a life."

"Only because you wanted his job."

Her retort struck a little too close for comfort. "I might be ambitious, but Kane is my brother. It bothered the entire family that he worked fourteen hour days. We're all glad he's so happy now with Beth," he explained stiffly.

They headed down the street again in silence, a silence that continued as they explored all three floors of the Huckleberry House.

"This place is enormous," Neil said finally, his irritation forgotten.

He was beginning to understand what Libby had immediately recognized; the house had tremendous potential. The echoes of a different, more gracious era whispered through the dusty rooms. Massive amounts of money had been poured into building the place, and he was quite certain a structural analysis would prove it was sound. Their biggest investment would be updating the plumbing and wiring.

In one of the bathrooms Neil tapped the ornate faucet handles and rubbed his fingers over inlaid marble on the floor. "This stuff has to be preserved as much as possible. We'll get the best craftsman in to work on it," he said, his thoughts moving swiftly. "I wonder if any of the furniture goes with the house. That would be great."

"It…would?" Libby asked faintly.

"Oh, yeah. We'll advertise we still have the original furnishings." He dragged a dustcover from a piece in the hallway, exposing a cherry wood whatnot table. "I wouldn't want this in my apartment, but it's great for a historic B and B."

"They say Teddy Roosevelt once stayed here," she murmured.

Perfect.

Adrenaline charged through Neil. He wanted to march right into town and put an option on the house before anyone else got the chance. It was an acceptable risk, and they could do a quick market analysis and structural inspection before the final papers were signed.

Taking out his cell phone, he redialed the real estate office, only to reach the answering machine.

"What about the other two properties you thought were possible?" he asked.

"They're close."

"Let's go," he said, striding down the stairs without a backward glance.

Libby dusted her hands and made a small face.

Endicott wasn't going to know what hit them.

By the time Neil had finished exploring the other two houses, he'd decided to put options on all three properties. They called the real estate office again, then Libby tried Ginger's home number.

"Ginger?" she said, relieved when her friend answered.

"Libby, I'm so sorry about rushing off like that. Harry is fine, it's just a sprain. He's already out playing in the yard."

"Are you coming back to the office? Mr. O'Rourke wanted to go over some details."

"I'll be there around four. I've got the evening shift at the pizza parlor, and Rob will be home by then to watch the kids."

Libby looked at Neil. "Is four all right?"

He nodded.

"All right, Ginger, we'll see you then."

Neil paced the street with restless energy. "That's two hours from now. What do you do in a place like this?"

Libby rubbed her forehead. There wasn't a single thing in Endicott that would interest a sophisticate like Neil O'Rourke. "I...um, could show you how Huckleberry House got its name. But it would require a short hike."

"Okay. Do you want to change clothes at your parents' house? I presume you keep stuff there."

"I'm a preacher's kid," she said, her stubborn chin lifting. "You get used to doing all kinds of things when you're dressed-up—you know, tidying up the sanctuary, serving coffee and washing dishes after the fellowship hour."

Neil smiled, imagining Libby as a youngster in her go-to-church dress, looking scrubbed and serious while she poured coffee and handed out cookies.

Ever since they'd arrived in Endicott she'd been baiting him with her background as a small-town preacher's daughter, expecting his disapproval. But he'd never known anyone who fitted into a place as naturally as Libby fitted into Endicott. It seemed as if she was loved and trusted by everyone in town.

The trail into the trees behind Huckleberry House was wide enough to walk side by side, and the whisper of their shoes on the forest floor melded with the twitter of birds and the scolding chirp of squirrels, upset by the intrusion of humans into their domain. He noticed that Libby climbed easily, though a drop of perspiration gleamed in the hollow of her throat.

It rolled downward, disappearing beneath her blouse, and Neil let out a pent-up breath.

Did she still wear a cotton bra, or had she switched to sexier lingerie along with her more stylish clothing? Libby's transformation from sweet preacher's daughter to assured businesswoman had been so gradual he'd hardly noticed it happening, but he couldn't ignore the fact that her new look drew a man's attention.

Especially *his* attention.

The gurgle of water ahead of him was a welcome distraction and his stride quickened until he realized that Libby couldn't keep up. He slowed and tried to quell his unruly thoughts.

To his surprise, a few minutes later she veered from the main path. Neil followed, twisting and turning along a trail that only Libby seemed able to see, his curiosity piqued. After a few hundred feet they pushed through a thicket of bushes until they reached the center of a small clearing, defined by a moss-covered fallen log.

Libby plucked several dark, bluish berries from one of the bushes and held out her hand. "They're small and late this year, but the flavor is good."

Eating wild fruit was new to Neil, and he looked at the bb-size berries on Libby's palm with a faint frown. He didn't think she disliked him enough to poison him, but there was always a chance she could make a mistake.

"What are they?"

"Huckleberries," she said.

"Ah, as in Huckleberry House."

"Yes. They grow all over the mountain, and used to cover the slope the house is built on. People say they're the best berry you can get. I make jam every year and I won first place at the town fair three years running for my huckleberry pie. That's when you have to retire as a competitor.''

Her hand shook, though she kept it extended. ''This is my own berry patch. I don't think anyone else knows it's here.''

''Aren't you worried I'll tell?''

Her shoulders lifted in an unconcerned shrug. ''Who would you tell?''

''And how would I find it again?'' Neil drawled. So this was one of her secret places; he felt like an intruder, even if she had invited him. ''That can't be the water I heard earlier.'' He motioned to a tiny trickle of water, falling into a pool that was a bare foot and a half across.

''It's a seep. Even in the driest years this one doesn't dry up. The water is pure—I can wash the berries if you'd prefer,'' she offered.

Neil smiled. ''They're fine just the way they are,'' he murmured. He caught her outstretched wrist, and before she could object, lowered his lips to the huckleberries.

He felt Libby's pulse quicken beneath his fingertips as he nibbled her offering into his mouth, berry by berry. He bit down on the small bits of fruit and flavor burst across his tongue. It was both sweet and tart and every bit as delicious as she'd promised.

''Wonderful,'' he said hoarsely.

What *was* it about Libby? He'd barely touched her and the top of his head was ready to come off…and that was nothing compared to the demanding pressure from another part of his anatomy.

Hell, he didn't even know what he was doing alone

on a mountain with her. Turning, Neil plucked a few of the berries. He could well imagine Libby patiently picking them, though it would take forever to get enough to make jam or a pie.

How many people would do something like that? No matter how great the reward?

Not many.

And he was certain that Libby freely gave the efforts of her labor away, to her family or friends. Her sweet nature had never been more evident than when she'd tried to preserve her mother's dignity by pretending that Faye—who was obviously somewhat frail—had really cooked their lunch.

"For you," he said, holding up a plump berry.

Her eyes widened further and her mouth opened in surprise. Neil slid the berry inside, his thumb brushing the velvet curves of her lips.

"Chew," he whispered.

Libby bit down automatically, barely tasting the fruit. What was Neil up to? She thought she recognized the heat in his eyes, but surely she was mistaken. They'd lost their heads that morning, a once-in-a-lifetime occurrence.

Well…*twice*-in-a-lifetime, if you counted their silly, best-forgotten date.

"Have another," Neil breathed.

She shivered and took a half step backward just as he released the berry. It disappeared into the deep V of her collar and her breath caught. Neil's gaze became heavy-lidded as he focused on the exact spot the berry had settled as if he could see through the fabric.

"You…I think you should, um…" her voice trailed off.

"Get it out of there. You're right," he said, deliberately misunderstanding. "It could leave a stain."

"Yes," Libby whispered.

She could stop him, but she didn't want to. Her nipples had tightened into tingly, aching knots—a sweet explosion of awareness. The last few days she'd felt more alive than she could ever remember feeling.

The rational part of her brain argued she was just excited about her promotion, only she wasn't so certain. She'd been promoted before, but she'd never matched wits with Neil. Going head-to-head with him was the last thing she'd expected to ever do, but it was curiously satisfying.

He lifted his finger and traced the path of the lost huckleberry, but when he dipped into her cleavage he didn't seem to be in any hurry to collect it, instead following the taut line of her bra.

"Silk. Nice," he whispered, his voice heavy with male satisfaction. "*Very* nice."

What? Libby felt vaguely insulted. "You're copping a feel of my bra? Don't tell me you have an underwear fetish, O'Rourke. I'd really be disappointed."

"It wouldn't be proper to cop a feel of anything else," he drawled with a self-directed, rueful humor. "Unless really provoked, of course."

Neil's finger slowly slid around the curve of her breast and located the lost berry. He scooped it out, regarded the tiny object for a long moment, then popped it into his mouth. "Delicious," he said, his voice sounding huskier than before. "I have a new favorite flavor."

Libby's knees wobbled.

She'd never seen the teasing, sensual side of Neil,

with every bit of his electric personality focused entirely on her. When they were younger he'd been brash, bold, cocky, wanting everything at light speed, but if this was how he'd learned to seduce women, no wonder they fell at his feet like swathes of wheat cut down by a sickle.

"What a curious expression you have," he said, brushing his thumb so lightly across her cheek it sent tingles through her nerves. "Am I the big bad wolf?"

"It wouldn't matter, I'm not Red Riding Hood," she quipped back, though her voice cracked, betraying her tension.

"Maybe. Maybe not. But…uh…getting back to our fascinating discussion this morning about kissing…"

"*Were* we getting back to that?"

Neil smiled. Libby had more spunk than he would have ever guessed. Adversity either destroyed people, or put steel into their backbones, and she'd come through her share of fire as pure, high-grade titanium.

"Yes. We never actually finished the experiment to see if a kiss would clear the air. In the interest of science we should test your theory."

Her eyes narrowed, almost imperceptibly. "That isn't why I brought you up here."

"Yeah, but you know men, we don't need a reason, we just need a place. And this one seems better than most."

"I said a *kiss* might clear the air, not sex," Libby snapped. This time her flush came from temper, and Neil knew she was more likely to hit him at the moment, than kiss him.

"You're right, sex would complicate things too

much. We'd better forget that part. I am, however, more than willing to kiss you."

"Neil O'Rourke, you are the most impossible man I've ever met. You can take anything I say and twist it to suit whatever you think is funny."

Hell.

He couldn't take it anymore. Libby's mouth was too tempting, and he *had* been copping a feel earlier, just like an underage boy with his britches on fire.

Clenching his hands at his sides, he leaned forward and kissed her.

Chapter Six

Libby didn't have time to think about responding before Neil stepped back again.

"What?"

"Just giving you time to hit me," he muttered.

"Hit you?"

"Yeah, for not asking first."

Was she mad about that? Libby tried to decide, then gave a mental shrug. He hadn't asked, but she also hadn't been saying no. Neil would never lose control and force her into something she didn't want. He'd stopped all those years ago, the moment she'd stiffened and pushed away from him.

Of course, he might not have been all that aroused that night, either.

The thought was too depressing for words.

She was an average woman, neither especially beautiful or particularly plain; wholesome was the best description for her. She ought to have married a guy from Endicott who'd appreciate wholesomeness, but it hadn't happened and now all her male friends were married to other women.

"I'm not going to hit you." She sighed and leaned against a moss covered tree trunk.

The little clearing wouldn't remain private once their B and B clients started arriving in Endicott. It wasn't the only huckleberry patch on the mountain, but she did love it. As a kid she'd come here to read and study, or just sit and dream about the future.

Libby closed her eyes and let the trees and water and wind whisper to her. She loved the Cascades, though life under an active volcano like Mount Rainier had its moments of concern. They weren't far from Mount Saint Helens…or what was left of the mountain after the top third had blown away in an eruption.

Soft, warm air disturbed the hair at her temple and Libby's eyelids shot open. Neil stood so close she could feel his body heat from her shoulders to her knees.

"Thought you'd forgotten me," he said, putting his hand on the tree above her head.

Forget him?

Not a chance.

Even if she wanted to.

"I was thinking about the mountain."

Neil glanced upward. The snow-shrouded monolith of Mount Rainier stood sentinel over them, a reminder that their lives were nothing but a flicker in the existence of the old giant.

"Never thought I'd be jealous of a mountain," he mused.

Libby made a huffy sound. "You aren't jealous. You have to actually *care* to be jealous."

"Of course I care—I just kissed a woman, but she's thinking about a mountain. A very attractive mountain to be sure, but it *is* just a mountain."

"Maybe you should do it again and get it right."

For a moment Neil wasn't sure he'd heard right. Libby, the preacher's daughter, sassing him over a kiss. His blood pressure went up a few notches.

"I always do like getting things right."

Yet he hesitated, wanting to be certain. It was pure madness pursuing any kind of personal contact with Libby, but he couldn't seem to help himself, not when she seemed equally interested.

"Neil…I, uh…"

The sound of his name was all he needed.

His mouth settled slowly, rubbing gently over Libby's in a chaste kiss that nevertheless sent blood rushing to the top of his thighs. He let it stay that way for a long moment, then stroked the seam of her lips with the tip of his tongue until she opened for him.

Yes.

Warning himself to go carefully, he explored deeper, tasting the lingering hint of huckleberry and something that seemed to be uniquely Libby.

Slim arms grasped his waist, then her hands moved up his chest, kneading and exploring like a curious cat.

Neil inhaled sharply and realized her perfume was far more subtle and complex than pure vanilla, it was a mixture of vanilla and spice and herbal scents that blended perfectly into a fresh, seductive whole.

He hadn't always enjoyed long, lingering kisses, seeing them merely as a prelude to the main event. But he liked them now. Slow, deep kisses that went on forever. Problem was, now that he'd started liking them that way, it seemed women were the ones in a hurry.

But not Libby.

She smelled good, tasted good, and oh my, did she kiss good.

Sometime in the past decade she'd picked up some experience in the kissing department, and a stab of jealousy left Neil wondering who might have been responsible. It was illogical and arrogant, but he was alone on a mountain with a woman who kissed like the first Eve and had the smile of a Christmas angel. Nothing about Libby was logical.

"Neil?"

"Hmmm?"

"Is it working?" she whispered between kisses.

"What?"

"Is the air getting cleared?" Libby asked, her head spinning. Here she was, kissing Neil O'Rourke again, something she'd sworn never to do, and liking it far too much.

"I think it'll take a little longer," he whispered. "And a little of this."

The "this" was obvious when his hand covered her right breast, thumb flicking over the sensitive peak. The tense, grabby sensation in Libby's abdomen suddenly got a lot worse, and she wriggled, hoping to make it go away.

Neil's other hand grasped her hip, halting her gyrations. "Don't *do* that," he growled.

"Do what?"

"Move."

"You don't like it?"

"Yeah, I like it." He backed away, dragging deep breaths into his lungs. "That was some experiment.

At least it got you to call me Neil, instead of Mr. O'Rourke.''

Neil.

She *had* called him by his first name, and Libby shook her head with anger. She didn't know who she was maddest at—Neil or herself. What an idiot she'd been. It wasn't as if she didn't know better.

''Then you win. I hope you're happy.''

''That's not what I meant.''

Neil winced at Libby's outraged expression as she spun and stalked out of the huckleberry patch. He started to straighten, then groaned; he was still aroused to the point of pain.

''Hey, I need a couple of minutes,'' he called after her, but she kept marching.

It was a while before he could stand straight without discomfort, and by then Libby was long gone. He didn't think he'd get lost on the way back to Huckleberry House—he wasn't that far from the old place—but he would have preferred a different end to their kiss.

''Damn,'' Neil muttered as he leaned over the small seep Libby had pointed out earlier, splashing water on his face and longing for a cold shower. He had a feeling he'd be taking a lot of them in the next few months if he kept working in such close contact with Libby.

Birds twittered in the trees above him and a squirrel scolded from a high perch, periodically tossing down pieces of a pine cone. They knew he didn't belong. It was just like in Endicott that morning, when he'd realized that somehow he was no longer in charge of the situation—a city slicker who didn't have a clue.

It wouldn't matter, except he was supposed to be starting a small town B and B line.

He was supposed to be starting the line?

Neil frowned.

Actually, that wasn't entirely true. He wasn't the only one responsible for the project, Libby shared in that responsibility and she knew small towns from the inside out. Like it or not, she could mean the difference between success and failure. It was a hard pill to swallow, because he'd always done things alone, his own way, and now he really needed someone else.

A glance at his wristwatch showed it was less than an hour before their appointment with the real estate agent. Trying to ignore the nagging ache in his groin, he followed the winding path out to the main trail, then down to Huckleberry House.

Libby sat on the sagging front step of the house, looking straight ahead.

"I might have gotten lost," he said to test her mood.

"It was only a quarter mile, I would have heard you bellow for help long before you really got lost."

Bellow?

Okay.

Her mood hadn't overly improved.

Neil stuck his hands in his pockets. "Libby, I didn't kiss you because I wanted to win something and it had nothing to do with getting you to stop calling me Mr. O'Rourke."

"Fine."

"It isn't fine. I didn't know what to say, and then I realized you'd called me Neil. I really liked it. Hell, you're right about me being stuffy at work," he admitted. "It's just hard knowing I'm good at my job, but having everyone think I'm only around because my brother owns the company.''

"Nobody thinks that."

Libby pressed the heels of her palms to her eyes, wishing she could stay angry. But she knew Neil hadn't meant to insult her, and the frustrated pride in his explanation struck a sympathetic chord inside her. She'd struggled at O'Rourke Enterprises in her own way.

"Everyone thinks I went from the typing pool to an executive position so quickly just because Kane likes me," she said finally. "Some of them probably think we were involved, though they're too polite to say so to my face."

"You know better."

"So do you. Does it help?"

"I guess not."

She stood up and grabbed the sweatshirt she'd been sitting on to protect her skirt. "Nobody thinks you aren't qualified, Neil. The whole company is in awe of the way you cut business deals. You're smart and decisive and don't have to prove yourself to a single person."

"Except to you."

Libby let out a humorless laugh and looked up. "You're the division president with a master's degree in business administration. I'm just a vice president with a fraction of your experience. I'm the one who has to prove myself, and I've done a lousy job of showing I'm capable."

Neil shook his head and she wished he wasn't so darned gorgeous. It didn't make sense. Looks were unimportant in the grand scheme of things, but here she was, weak in the knees over a tough-minded businessman with a cash register for a heart.

Of course, his biological responses seemed perfectly normal.

Very normal.

Maybe he was human after all.

"You haven't messed anything up, quite the opposite," he said. "All day long I've been trying to pretend I know what I'm doing here, but the truth is, I don't have a clue. People like and trust you, they talk to you. That's going to be as valuable on this project as anything I have to contribute. I'd like to believe I can do it all, but that isn't realistic."

He seemed sincere, but Libby knew that sooner or later he'd remember she was the one who'd talked about them kissing, and things would be worse than ever when they got back to Seattle.

Jeez, why had she opened her mouth?

"I'm the one who suggested we could clear the air by…"

"Kissing?"

Great, she'd gone and opened her mouth again. Wasn't that just swell? She'd be lucky to have a job tomorrow.

"You wouldn't have thought about it if I hadn't said I was still attracted to you, and I'm the one who brought it up again. So let's accept equal blame," Neil said quietly. "Besides, you didn't suggest anything I hadn't already been thinking about."

"Oh." Libby swallowed at the dark heat in his eyes.

"We'll just have to go about our business and try not to let it happen again." He looked at his watch, adjusted his tie, and stomped some dust from his shoes. "It's three forty-five. Let's go meet with that real estate agent."

Libby—her head already whirling from his statement that they would have to "try" not to let another kiss happen—nodded.

Try not to let it happen?

Did that mean Neil O'Rourke wasn't completely sure about something?

That evening Libby turned into her long driveway and pressed the button of her automatic garage door opener. Thanks to her generous salary, she'd recently been able to purchase a fifteen acre lot up in the hills. Endicott was too far for commuting, but at least she lived outside of the city now.

The two-story house looked out on a small natural lake, surrounded by woods. So far the remaining lots hadn't been developed by the owner, so she didn't have any close neighbors. It suited her. She loved the peace and quiet and the animals that came to drink at the lake…though right now it seemed awfully lonely.

She let herself into the house and her cat, Bilbo, abruptly leapt into her arms.

"Lord, you have to give me more warning," Libby scolded softly, staggering slightly beneath the feline's twenty-nine pounds of muscles and energy. Bilbo was a lovable goofball who snuggled with her at night and complained loudly when she left in the morning.

His purr rumbled out and she sat down with him draped over her stomach and arms.

Neil had put options on all three of the houses they'd looked at, options held with his personal check. He'd begun haggling over the price on the properties until she'd kicked him under the table. The asking price was dirt cheap, and getting them any cheaper wouldn't benefit their second goal of community development.

"I kicked him, Bilbo," Libby mumbled.

The feline butted her chin and she scratched his neck.

"After everything that happened, I lost my cool and kicked him. Of course, he deserved to be kicked," she added quickly. "The price was more than fair."

"Maarrroow."

"I know, Neil is in charge, and I should have been more subtle."

With a sensuous twist of his body, Bilbo turned over on his back, his legs sprawling in four directions. He wasn't much on subtlety, either.

Libby leaned back and closed her eyes. After spending the day with Neil her emotions and peace of mind were twisted beyond recognition. What surprised her the most was the way he was trying to accept her advice and make changes in the way he did things.

She hadn't thought Neil was capable of change.

The fact that he seemed to be trying was encouraging. They might be able to work together after all, though she must have lost her mind to suggest that a kiss would diminish their attraction. Her body hummed with awareness, worse than before, and she fairly ached to have his hands on her body.

"Nothing worse than a frustrated virgin," she grumbled to Bilbo.

He let out a faint snore. Now that she was home, the essential ingredients to his happiness were complete—food, a warm place to sleep, and unconditional

love. If he could get two of them in the same place—
Libby's lap—then he was in cat heaven.

Careful not to disturb the snoozing feline, Libby
kicked off her shoes and willed herself to relax.

A little rebellion was natural. She'd worked hard
and always tried to do the right thing, now she wanted
to explore the part of her life she'd neglected. No
orgies, just a little old-fashioned heat and sizzle under
the blankets with the right man.

Instead she'd gone and kissed the wrong man.

She really didn't have this rebellion thing worked
out too well.

By Thursday Libby was getting restless. Her body
still hummed when she came within twenty feet of
Neil and she'd dreamed every night of that heated
moment in the huckleberry patch.

Sighing, she opened the market analysis they'd re-
quested from the research staff. There weren't any
surprises; it said there was great potential in Endicott
for one or more bed-and-breakfast inns, which Neil
had probably already guessed.

Getting up she went to his office next door, only
to stop when she saw that Margie Clarke's personal
belongings were absent. Libby took an envelope from
the corner of Margie's desk and saw "Neil
O'Rourke" scrawled across it.

Swell.

She knocked and went in when he called out.

"I finished reading the market report," she said.

Neil smiled at Libby. He was still struggling with
his reaction to her, but he was pretty sure she didn't
know about it. "Why didn't Margie let me know you
were waiting?"

NO POSTAGE
NECESSARY
IF MAILED
IN THE
UNITED STATES

BUSINESS REPLY MAIL
FIRST-CLASS MAIL   PERMIT NO. 717-003   BUFFALO, NY

POSTAGE WILL BE PAID BY ADDRESSEE

SILHOUETTE READER SERVICE
3010 WALDEN AVE
PO BOX 1867
BUFFALO NY 14240-9952

Get FREE BOOKS and a FREE GIFT when you play the...

LAS VEGAS
GAME

Just scratch off the gold box with a coin. Then check below to see the gifts you get!

YES! I have scratched off the gold Box. Please send me my **2 FREE BOOKS** and **gift for which I qualify**. I understand that I am under no obligation to purchase any books as explained on the back of this card.

© 2001 HARLEQUIN ENTERPRISES LTD.
® and TM are trademarks owned by Harlequin Enterprises Ltd.

309 SDL DVCF   209 SDL DVCL

FIRST NAME	LAST NAME

ADDRESS

APT.#	CITY

STATE/PROV.	ZIP/POSTAL CODE

(S-R-01/04)

Visit us online at
www.eHarlequin.com

7	**7**	**7**	Worth TWO FREE BOOKS plus a BONUS Mystery Gift!
🍒	🍒	🍒	Worth TWO FREE BOOKS!
🔔	🔔	♣	TRY AGAIN!

Offer limited to one per household and not valid to current Silhouette Romance® subscribers. All orders subject to approval.

"Because she isn't here. All her things are gone, and I found this on her desk." Libby handed him the envelope.

Inside was a resignation letter, effective immediately.

"*Dammit.* Why didn't she just talk to me? I could have had another secretary up here by now."

"Probably because she knew that would be your response," Libby said dryly. "How it would affect you. Margie has other things on her mind besides your feelings, like a daughter with kidney failure who isn't responding well to dialysis."

Neil swallowed a flash of embarrassment; he didn't enjoy the feeling he'd come up short in Libby's eyes. "I asked her if everything was all right."

Libby gave him an inscrutable look. "No doubt in a tone of voice that said you'd commit hari kari if she actually told you what was wrong."

Ouch.

That was true.

Hell, he wasn't good with the one-on-one, touchy-feely sort of stuff. On the other hand, Libby was a preacher's daughter who excelled in "touchy-feely."

"Er…Libby, I don't suppose you could…?"

"Talk to Margie?"

"Yeah. I don't want her to quit because of her daughter. If she needs time off, of course she can have it."

It would be a pain, especially with the reorganization of the company starting so soon, though Neil couldn't blame Margie. He usually figured someone's personal life should stay out of the office, but when your kid was critically ill… Nobody could be expected to keep *that* out of the office.

"All right. I'll contact her this afternoon."

Libby made a notation on her pad, pleased Neil was making an effort to be understanding. A few weeks ago he would have handled things much differently.

"By the way, Kane says I should pick an assistant as part of my new position," Libby said. "Maybe I can take Margie, and you can work with someone else who doesn't have family issues."

His jaw tightened. "You don't think I can be sensitive enough with her, do you?"

Personally, Libby thought Neil had the sensitivity of a brick, but it wouldn't help to say so. He might be trying to change, but he had a long way to go before he qualified as boss of the year.

"If Margie decides to come back, she'd probably be more comfortable with me, especially on days when she has to call in unexpectedly," she said. She was congratulating herself on how carefully she'd spoken when Neil shook his head.

"No. It's my problem. Just convince her to come back. Someone else can handle her workload when she has to be gone."

Libby's took several breaths to help her calm down. The man was so dense. How he could have such a brilliant business mind and still not have a *clue,* she didn't know.

"Margie is the one with a problem, not you. How do you expect her to feel if you approach her with that attitude?"

"Just tell—"

"If you want Margie to come back, *you* tell her. Say you didn't know about her daughter, that you understand how rough it is, and want to be part of the solution, not the problem," Libby said furiously.

"She doesn't need to feel guilty right now because *you're* inconvenienced."

Neil leaned back in his chair, fascinated. Libby's chest rose and fell with anger, her green eyes were the color of flawless emeralds, and a pink flush that had nothing to do with shy embarrassment was flooding her cheeks.

"All right," he said. "I'll talk to Margie."

"You...will?" She sounded surprised.

"Yes. You don't think I can do it. I'll show you I can."

The anger fled Libby's eyes, yet it seemed to have been replaced by disappointment.

What the hell had he done wrong now?

Chapter Seven

Before Neil could ask Libby what was wrong, she shrugged. "I see," she murmured. "Do you want to talk about the market analysis for Endicott?"

He wanted to know why she looked so disappointed, yet at the same time he *didn't* want to know why her good opinion mattered so much to him. It was just like the other night; she'd said goodbye very politely, then thanked him for being nice to her parents.

What had she expected, he'd be *rude* to them?

Was that why she'd been so reluctant to have lunch with her mom and dad? He'd spent hours wondering what she'd meant about being "nice," when he should have been thinking about other things.

"Actually, I just heard from Kane," Neil said. "He likes our ideas on setting up the division. And we have accounts established now for the B and B project, so we can go ahead and start acquiring properties and contracting for the necessary work."

Libby nodded, her face showing no emotion what-soever. "That's good. I talked to Endicott Construc-tion this morning. They're interested in a contract for Huckleberry House as long as we get a restoration specialist to consult with them. Have you decided anything about the other two houses? I presume we're going ahead on Huckleberry House since both the market report and structural analysis were positive."

He remained silent for a long minute.

"Neil?"

"Yeah, I've made up my mind."

It probably wasn't the best decision to acquire all three properties in Endicott, so he'd decided to take the largest two for the company, and keep the third as a weekend retreat unless they decided it would be needed.

The thought of something so rural would have dis-mayed him before he'd gone on that scouting trip with Libby, but he was seeing things differently now. There was a peace in the mountains, a flow of natural rhythms that were older than the ice-capped peaks, and just as strong.

He could always sell or lease the house if he changed his mind, or discovered he didn't use it. Giv-ing into an impulse of the moment wasn't like him, but he'd never experienced a more erotic moment than when he'd eaten that huckleberry, warm and scented from Libby's breast.

Damn.

Neil groaned silently. No matter how often he swore he wouldn't think about their kiss, he couldn't stop remembering. If Libby knew she'd slap his face so hard she'd hurt her hand, then say something sarcastic about his obsession with sex. He didn't know, maybe men *did* think about sex more than women.

"And…?" Libby prompted, yanking him back to the cool sterility of his office. "Which ones are we buying?"

"Huckleberry House and the place on Salish street," he murmured. "I can't believe we're getting them for so little."

"You still wanted to dicker the price down further."

"Yeah, but I shut up when you kicked me."

A light pink flush spread across her cheeks. "I just thought…that is, we're supposed to be thinking about community revitalization as well as starting the line of inns, so it didn't seem like a good idea to get sticky about an already fair price."

"You were right," Neil acknowledged and watched her eyes widen.

There were a number of things he struggled with, and admitting he was wrong was one of them. Yet somehow it seemed easier with Libby. Maybe because he'd already told her how it felt to be the boss's brother, always needing to prove himself.

Or maybe it was because she'd declared so adamantly that he didn't have anything to prove. He didn't think it was true—especially when it came to her—but it was nice to hear. Besides, he had a feeling the things he needed to prove to Libby had less to do with business, more to do with something more personal.

"Let's work out the itinerary for our next few scouting trips," he said.

An hour later Libby looked at the clock and

stretched. "It's lunchtime. Can we finish this later? I need to do some errands."

"Of course."

He would have liked to suggest they order a meal brought in and keep working, but Libby had a great deal of responsibility in her private life. He didn't want to put her in the position of explaining what her errands were about, and whether they could be put off until another day.

But it wasn't until the door had closed behind her that Neil realized he'd put Libby's priorities ahead of his own, *and* ahead of the business.

A soft whistle issued through his lips.

The world seemed to be settling into a different orbit, with the scent of Libby's perfume streaming behind it like a jet's vapor trail.

And all at once he understood her disappointment earlier over what he'd said about Margie Clarke. Margie's problems weren't about him, and showing he could handle it satisfactorily wasn't the point. The point was to help a loyal and hardworking employee deal with a devastating crisis.

Neil opened the company's personnel roster and found Margie's name and home phone number.

He quickly punched the buttons and waited.

"Margie?" he said when she answered. "This is Neil O'Rourke. I want to discuss how we can help you through a tough time. But let's talk about something even more important first…how is your daughter doing?"

Libby hurried into her office and smiled at the building guard who'd insisted on carrying her parcels up from the lobby.

"Put those down anywhere, Ted. I appreciate the help."

"Delighted, Libby. Though I have to admit I feel a little funny carrying bags from some of these stores." Ted grinned and set everything down on her desk.

She couldn't blame him. He was a burly, six-foot-four-inch security specialist who'd probably felt silly carrying the very feminine shopping bags with their dainty handles, pastel colors and trailing tissue paper.

"This stuff is for Jeanine's wedding shower tomorrow," she said, "so don't say a word. I'm in charge of the party and it's supposed to be a surprise."

"My lips are sealed."

As he walked out Libby flopped down into a chair and fanned herself. Though the weather had turned cool, she'd rushed so quickly through her shopping she felt warm and flushed. Or maybe it was thinking about the personal item she'd gotten at the exclusive lingerie store at the same time she'd picked out her gift to Jeanine.

She had zero need for a green silk nightgown that exposed more skin that it covered. It was elegant, but it clung and scooped and drew attention to areas she normally wanted concealed. Nightgowns like that weren't for wearing alone, they were designed to please a man. Of course, some women would say that was a sexist attitude and you should dress to please yourself.

"Women's lib be darned," Libby said. Sometimes a woman dressed to please a man, it was as simple as that.

Except the only male who would see her in that

nightgown was a twenty-nine pound feline who wouldn't care what it "almost" revealed.

"Boy, is that pathetic, or what?" She was trying to decided *how* pathetic when her phone rang.

"Libby Dumont, New Developments Division," she said.

"Hi, Libby, this is Margie."

Margie sounded brighter than she had in weeks, but Libby didn't have time to collect her thoughts before the other woman rushed on.

"I just got off the phone with Neil and he was so wonderful. We talked for over an hour, and he's going to call a renal specialist he knows in New York to go over Sally's medical files. I couldn't imagine talking to him for even five minutes before, but it was so comfortable. He said not to worry when I couldn't make it to work, that I should just leave a message if I can't reach him and then let personnel know so they could send someone up to cover the phones. Isn't that great of him?"

"Uh...yes."

Libby listened in stunned silence as Margie gave a blow-by-blow description of her conversation with Neil, mixed with accolades about her new boss who apparently had developed the ability to walk on water.

Neil?

They were talking about the same Neil O'Rourke who turned up his nose about marriage and acted as if a spouse and children would be the biggest sacrifice of his life?

That Neil?

She didn't want to have any warmer feelings toward him than absolutely necessary, but a treacherous sensation crept around Libby's heart as she realized he'd not only convinced Margie to return, he'd made her feel better.

For a long time after she said goodbye, Libby sat and stared at the parcels she'd rushed to get. Several of her co-workers had offered to take over planning for the wedding shower now that she'd been promoted, but she'd insisted on doing a lot of it. A cake and other food would be delivered for the party tomorrow, but she'd needed to get the decorations and favors so they could decorate tonight.

"A lot on your mind?"

The question startled her so much she nearly fell off her chair. "What are you doing here?" she demanded, glaring at Neil.

"I thought we could keep working on our various travel itineraries," he said smoothly, though a wicked smile curved his mouth as he lifted the bag from the lingerie store with one finger. "One of your errands?"

Heat suffused Libby's face and it was all she could do not to snatch the large silver bag away from him. "It's a wedding shower present. Jeanine Garber is getting married so we're throwing a party for her."

"Jeanine?"

"Yes. She and her fiancé were the ones in that awful accident during the summer. It's a miracle they survived."

"Oh, right, I remember." Neil poked in the bag and lifted a cloud of green silk into the air. "Very nice, but I thought Jeanine had blue eyes."

Trust Neil O'Rourke to remember the color of a woman's eyes, but not to recall if she had children or know anything else about her except her waist and bust size.

"Are they?" There was no way in creation she'd admit the nightgown was for her, not Jeanine.

"Yes. Didn't they have any blue ones?"

"I don't remember," she lied. Honestly, Neil was terrible for her morals. She'd never fibbed so much in her life before they'd been assigned to work together. She only hoped he wouldn't also open the silver gift box that contained a blue negligee set.

"This is nice." He lifted the gown higher, so the sheer draped silk over the bodice became obvious. "Really nice. I'm probably not invited to the shower, but I'd like to contribute toward the gift."

"That's all right," Libby said hastily, giving into temptation and grabbing both the bag and green silk away from him. "But this is a personal gift from me to Jeanine."

"I'd still like to contribute. That's a very pretty nightgown—perfect for a shower gift, I imagine."

It was a sexy, utterly wicked nightgown, and he was just using it to tease her since he obviously didn't believe she'd buy something so provocative for herself. Not Libby Dumont, the preacher's daughter. Even though her friends and family would make the same assumption, it seemed worse having Neil think so.

"I may keep it for myself and give Jeanine something else," she said impulsively.

"Really?"

Neil kept from grinning with an effort. It had only taken a single glance at Libby's embarrassed pink cheeks to realize the "shower" gift wasn't a gift at all. Honestly, there was something about her that kept making him want to ruffle her up. It wasn't professional, and he had a sneaking suspicion it was also downright immature. At thirty-five he shouldn't have such foolish impulses.

"Really." She stuffed the green silk out of sight and shoved the bag beneath her desk. "I'll meet you in your office in a few minutes so we can go back to work."

Neil nodded and left, though it was mostly self-preservation because he'd just gotten another immature impulse…imagining how Libby would look wearing nothing more than a cloud of green silk and perfume.

Only there was nothing about *that* idea that made him want to laugh.

Chapter Eight

"What do you think?" the real estate agent asked.

They were on the first day of a three day swing through southern Washington and northern Oregon, and Libby stared at the building in front of her, trying to think of a polite way to say it was awful.

Awful didn't begin to cover it.

Though the house had sat empty for a long time, it was in reasonably good shape. There were several bathrooms on each of the main floors, but it was the sheer dreariness of the uninspired boxlike structure that made it impossible.

"Good, solid construction," the man said a little too heartily. "And a good price."

"Libby?" Neil prompted.

"It looks like a factory," she whispered too low for the agent to hear."

"Well, it *was* a factory. Sort of."

Libby didn't have to look at Neil to know he was trying not to laugh. Yeah, the house had been "sort of'' a factory. A *sex* factory. According to Bob Haney, the real estate agent, it had operated as a brothel before being turned into an even more dreary boardinghouse. He'd probably revealed that small bit of early history in a desperate attempt to make it sound more intriguing than it really was.

"It would certainly make for interesting advertising,'' she murmured. "Though we might have trouble drawing the family trade with it.''

Neil choked and pretended to look at the cracked sidewalk. Not long ago he would have expected Libby to put her back up and get huffy about being shown a former brothel, but he was learning she had a great sense of humor as long as he didn't get her riled up first.

As for the former brothel…

He shook his head. Of course, this was one of the real estate agents he'd dealt with himself. Maybe if Libby had called she could have charmed the guy into showing them something more appropriate.

"Mr. O'Rourke?'' Bob Haney prompted.

"It really doesn't meet our needs,'' he said bluntly.

The man's face fell. He'd probably carried the listing for years and had hoped he was finally going to get someone blind or dumb enough to fork over the money.

"Mr. Haney, as we drove out here I noticed a house by a little stream,'' Libby said, smiling at the agent. "Your office's name was on the sign. Can you tell us something about it?''

"Oh, you mean the old Wilton place. You won't find it suitable. There have been several different additions to the house, none of them very well planned. It's too big for a single family home and too much of a maze for a business." Haney was so dispirited he didn't even attempt to sound encouraging.

"I'd love to see it."

While he plainly considered it a waste of his time, he asked them to follow and got into his own car.

"I almost feel sorry for him," Neil said, grinning broadly as he helped Libby into the Blazer.

"It must be hard making a living around here," she observed, far more sympathetically.

But that was Libby. She had a kind heart, though he'd discovered she wasn't letting it get in the way of business. As a matter of fact, she seemed to have an extraordinary ability to look beyond sagging porches and peeling paint to see if true gold lay beneath…and to get him to see that gold.

He'd learned to watch her green eyes, and knew if she got that dreamy expression on her face they were in luck. In the past two weeks they'd discovered seven additional properties for the project, and work would begin soon on them.

Neil followed Haney's car as he turned around and headed back toward the river. They'd ordered market analyses on the various towns they'd be scouting, eliminating some communities because there was nothing promising in the reports. As it turned out, there were a lot of towns in Oregon and Washington he'd never even heard of, much less visited.

Curiously, he was feeling a great satisfaction in the project. It wasn't the large scale he was accustomed to working at, but it didn't seem to matter. He was even thinking about expanding beyond the Pacific northwest—the gold country in California sounded interesting, and he'd bet there were great places on the east coast to start bed-and-breakfast inns.

Of course, it might just be Libby's enthusiasm about the whole thing.

He'd never had a partner in the international branch. He'd just done what was necessary and answered to his brother alone. But with Libby...he found himself picking up the phone to ask her opinion on something he was working on, only to realize it was late at night and he'd have to wait until the next day.

Since it was unsettling to think about how often that had happened, Neil motioned to the road ahead of them.

"I don't remember seeing this house you asked about."

"You were busy driving."

They pulled into a circular driveway with a rambling house set well back from the road. The surrounding area was nice, rather pastoral, with rolling hills and trees leaning over a winding stream. But the house...he shook his head. Someone in the distant past had painted the place a bright yellow with turquoise trim that made it look more like a clown's home than a candidate for an elegant bed-and-breakfast inn.

"White," Libby murmured. "With dark green trim. Not black, that would be too stark."

She had that look, and Neil wondered why it gave him a warm sensation clear through his chest. It wasn't even professional of her to reveal so much, because a real estate agent would guess she'd fallen in love and was ripe to spend more money than a place was worth.

He didn't care.

Which just proved he was losing an edge in his

thinking, though there were worse things that could happen. Neil wasn't certain when he'd come to that conclusion, but he was pretty sure Libby was responsible.

"It'll take more than one coat of paint to cover that yellow," he said. "It's practically neon."

Libby flashed him a smile that sent another shaft of warmth through him. "We'll just use a good primer."

"We will, huh?"

Getting out he walked around to the passenger side of the Blazer. There'd been a couple times she'd jumped out on her own, until he'd bluntly announced it would "look" better if he acted like a gentleman and helped her in and out of the car.

Neil didn't actually care what anyone else thought, but no matter how hard he tried to be a modern guy, he'd been taught to behave a certain way with women. His sisters all rolled their eyes and complained about the O'Rourke atavistic male tendencies, yet nothing could change him. And with Libby there was the added bonus of getting to touch her.

He could tell she was uncomfortable with the ritual, but it didn't make sense. Didn't those country boys she'd grown up with have manners? His father had taught him about watching his mouth and standing in a lady's presence by the time he was two years old. Keenan O'Rourke had followed a code his entire life, a code that said you took care of your family and acted a certain way because that's what being a man was all about. Neil hadn't thought about his father's code for a long time, but it was still firmly engrained in him.

"Little towns are old-fashioned. They'll refuse to

do business with us if I don't behave well," he said again.

"Really?" she asked dryly.

"Really."

"You don't know anything about small towns."

"I can't deny it, not with you reminding me every five minutes."

Libby cast a glance at Neil, but saw he was smiling. His gray eyes didn't look nearly as cool as usual and her silly heart did a flip flop. He could be nice when he wanted to be, even when he wasn't trying to charm his way into a woman's bloomers.

"Mr. O'Rourke, Miss Dumont, do you want to see inside?" Mr. Haney gestured toward the front door, which was painted in white and black zebra stripes. The last owner had unique taste, to say the least.

Libby half-closed her eyes and envisioned how it would look with a shiny all-white door and wrought-iron fixtures.

Lovely.

She gulped when a hand settled low on her back, warm and firm. As many times as Neil had done that on their day trips around Seattle, and today as they had headed south, she wasn't accustomed to it. She also wasn't accustomed to the idea they'd be spending three whole days together—separate motel rooms at night, naturally, but aside from that they'd be rarely outside of the other's company.

"What are you thinking about?" his voice whispered in her ear, his breath lifting a strand of hair.

Lord…she didn't know, her brain felt scrambled by sensory overload. "Um…about my cat. I can't remember if I brought up enough canned food for my parents to feed him."

Oh, that was good.

Now she sounded like a lonely spinster fussing over having enough tuna to treat her only companion.

"I'm sure it's fine." Neil's fingers moved subtly, like a caress, and tingles spread out in concentric circles. The muscles in her bottom and abdomen tightened and she stumbled slightly.

"S-sorry," she gasped.

"The ground is uneven here. As for the cat, I'll bet your mother is spoiling him rotten," Neil assured, moving closer so more of her brain cells could short circuit.

"Uh…right."

Her parents would be much happier babysitting grandchildren instead of a huge Maine Coon cat who wandered around their house in a moody funk whenever she was gone. Libby didn't know why she'd even said something about Bilbo, yet all sorts of things came out of her mouth these days that surprised the heck out of her.

Part of it she understood.

For some unaccountable reason she felt freer with Neil than any other man she'd ever known. She could say what she wanted without repercussions. He wasn't a member of her father's church who expected her to behave a certain way. It was obvious there wouldn't be any professional backlash if she spoke her mind, and despite their kiss on the mountain, they weren't romantically involved. Or ever would be. His behavior had been irritatingly proper ever since, even if he had teased her over that green silk nightgown.

But there wasn't any reason to keep reminding Neil that she was a twenty-nine-year-old unmarried preacher's daughter.

Unless…

A disturbing thought occurred to Libby. Unless she wanted him to revert to that overbearing, obnoxious and arrogant man she'd always known so she could safely dismiss him, getting infatuated with a man like Neil O'Rourke was the dumbest thing a woman could do.

"What's your cat's name?" he asked, perversely doing the exact opposite of what she wanted.

"Bilbo."

"Really?" Neil grinned, looking younger and more carefree than she'd ever seen him. "Bilbo is a character from those books by Tolkien, right? I loved the *Lord of the Rings* trilogy when I was a kid. I'd completely forgotten."

"Yes, but *The Hobbit* is my favorite," Libby admitted before she could think better of it. The idea of Neil reading the richly complex fantasies by J.R.R. Tolkien was astonishing.

"This house almost looks like something out of *The Hobbit,*" he said softly. "All it needs is a thatch roof and a good paint job. We could call it the Shire and encourage hobbit and elven wannabes to come visit. Don't you think that's a great idea for a bed-and-breakfast inn?"

He might have been talking nonsense for all she knew. His hand had cupped her hip, sending the last vestige of rational thought from her head. Did he realize what he was doing?

Mr. Haney pointedly cleared his throat, bringing Libby back to earth. "The electricity is off inside. But I have a flashlight."

From the corner of her eye she saw Neil's imperiously raised eyebrow and her mouth twitched. He was annoyed at the interruption, which was peculiar since it was business that had interrupted them.

"I'm sure we'll be able to manage," she said.

Light filtered through the arching tree branches high above them and a few dry leaves left from the late fall rustled in the breeze. Inside the house the sun proved low enough to send a golden glow into the western windows, and she prowled around with growing delight.

The rooms were small but charming, with odd corners and twists and turns of passageways that were reminiscent of a rabbit warren—with an English country cottage flavor. But they could capitalize on that. Brer Rabbit, Peter Cottontail, and J.R.R. Tolkien's hobbits would be right at home in the cozy place. Everything should be homey, like strawberry jam and lemonade on hot summer days. They could serve English tea and scones in the sunny sitting room, and put brass beds in the bedrooms, piled high with pillows and thick comforters.

"Brass beds, eh?" Neil stood with his hands in his pockets, head cocked quizzically.

With a start Libby realized she'd been talking aloud, and heat flooded her face. "If we decide the house is what we want, of course."

Bob Haney, who was looking much brighter than before, nodded eagerly. "You have some wonderful ideas, Miss Dumont. You're so right, this would make a fine bed-and-breakfast inn. And the town would benefit so much from a successful business."

Drat.

Neil would be furious, thinking she'd driven the price up unnecessarily. Why hadn't he kicked her? She'd kicked *him* when he was doing something she thought was a mistake. But no, he probably preferred yelling at her.

"I agree, Mr. Haney. And we'd love to hear your ideas about the community," Neil said calmly.

Libby's jaw dropped.

"You would?" asked the real estate agent.

"Absolutely. I'm sure you have insight into what would help the most."

The agent's face melted into a genuine smile, far different than the professional, I'm-going-to-be-cheerful-no-matter-what sort of grimace he'd been hiding behind. He launched into a description of everything he thought would help Griffith, the town he'd apparently lived in his entire life. Neil not only listened, he took out his notebook and started jotting items down and asking more questions.

Deciding she wasn't needed, Libby continued exploring the old house, but her mind was barely on it.

Neil had her so confused she couldn't sleep at night.

He hadn't said a word about talking with his secretary about her sick daughter, though he'd led Libby to believe he was only doing it to prove he could be "sensitive." She'd tried to say something about it, but he'd changed the subject so quickly she'd barely gotten three words out.

Margie had been completely won over, and Libby worried the single mother was getting a serious crush on him.

Except for his initial dismay, Neil had thrown himself into the bed-and-breakfast inn project with his usual pedal to the metal style.

And it turned out that he had a sense of humor, too, darn it.

Opening the back door, she stepped out into a flagstone patio and garden, now a wild tangle of growth, but once the recipient of loving attention. She followed the path to an ancient lily pond, where assorted ducks cheerfully paddled and quacked.

"This is nice, but shouldn't the ducks have migrated by now?" asked Neil as he walked down the path toward her.

Libby lifted her shoulders. "I think they're year-round residents. Are we going back to the real estate office?"

"We'll see Mr. Haney first thing in the morning. He'll have the papers ready by then."

She hesitated, still wondering if he was angry. "Are you mad?"

"About what?"

"You know, about...the brass beds and stuff. I know it isn't a good idea to let a real estate agent know we're excited about a property, but I didn't realize what I was talking to myself."

Neil looked at Libby, astonished.

Mad?

How could he be mad?

At himself, maybe, for losing his perspective when it came to her and doing business, but not about the cute way she forgot herself and thought out loud. If he'd been mad about *that* he would have gagged her after the first house they'd looked at outside of Endicott.

"No, I'm not mad." Unable to resist, he put out his hand and brushed a lock of hair from her cheek.

Wanting to ask her opinion about something wasn't all he thought about late in the evening; he also thought about her sweet, sassy mouth and the kindness she showed everyone. He woke up several times a night thinking her scent was clinging to his pillow and wishing it was real. For a guy who prided himself on keeping his private and business life separate, he was doing a lousy job.

"Neil?"

"Mr. Haney left already," he whispered. "I think we just made his year buying this place."

"Why aren't you mad?" she persisted.

He sighed. No wonder his mother liked Libby; they were both equally stubborn.

"I can't explain it," Neil admitted, letting his hand fall to his side. "You get excited like that and I know we've found a winner. I figure I can keep the business dealings sorted out."

Her eyes darkened. "You have to keep it sorted out because I'm so *un*businesslike. That's what you meant."

Sheesh. He let out a breath. "Every time I think we're past this nonsense, it comes back. I admit in the beginning I did think you weren't the best choice as vice president, but I quickly discovered I was wrong."

"Really."

It wasn't a comment, more a statement of disbelief, and Neil scowled.

"Yes, really. And if you had any idea how much I hate saying I was wrong, then you wouldn't be so skeptical." It might be easier telling Libby he was wrong than admitting it to other people, but it still didn't go down comfortably. Especially since he had this nagging compulsion to win her good opinion.

"All right."

All right?

Was that some kind of feminine set up, a trap waiting to be sprung on him? With four younger sisters he'd learned there were an inexhaustible supply of those traps, just waiting to trip you up when you least expect it.

"You want to run that by me again?" Neil asked cautiously.

Libby shrugged. "It's all right. I'm getting hungry. Do you feel like pizza?"

She turned and headed up the path toward the front of the house, and Neil's scowl deepened. That wasn't the end of it. It was never the end. Once a woman became more than a business partner she could mess with your mind, and like it or not, Libby was more than a business partner. Kissing her had made certain of that.

Except…it *did* seem to be the end of it.

At the pizza parlor Libby slid across the cracked leatherette of a booth and smiled happily. "This looks like Ginger's pizza place."

Neil was considerably less enthusiastic. "Maybe we should check out the Chinese restaurant."

A perky waitress in a tight T-shirt and even tighter jeans walked up just then. She was tall, leggy, and her belly button showed, and Libby glanced wryly down at her more conservative outfit. Neil had suggested they wear more casual clothing on their scouting trips, so she'd chosen an eyelet blouse and full skirt to make it easier getting in and out of the Blazer. They were pretty and feminine, but hardly sexy.

"Hi," said the waitress. "My name is Sue. May I help you?"

"Do you have any specialties?" Neil asked doubtfully.

"Just what's on the menu." Sue motioned to folded sheets of paper stuck between the napkin holder and a shaker holding crushed dried red pepper.

"I love your necklace," Libby said quickly, directing a dire glance at Neil. They weren't going to find some gourmet pasta with gorgonzola cheese and portabella mushrooms in a small town pizza joint.

The waitress touched the silver Celtic knot at her throat and nodded. "Thanks. My dad made it. He got hurt working as a logger, so he's trying his hand at jewelry. Not that there's much market around here for that sort of thing."

Libby looked at Neil in time to see a flicker of pain in his eyes, and knew he'd been reminded of his own father who had died working for a logging company.

"Er…what do you recommend?" she asked, pulling out one of the menus. They seemed to have a variety of selections, not all of them pizza.

"It's all good, except Tucker's Italian chicken. If you ask me, Italy should sue Tuck for calling it Italian."

"I heard that," shouted a voice from the back.

Sue chuckled. "My husband makes great pizza, but he's got no sense of humor when it comes to his cooking."

"Do you like pepperoni, or what?" Libby asked Neil. His face had frozen into an expressionless mask and she wished she'd never mentioned the other woman's necklace.

"We could put some artichoke hearts on if regular pizza's not special enough for you," Sue offered. "I'm sure we've got a jar of them back there someplace." She gave Libby a wink.

Libby coughed, torn between laughter and sadness.

Neil still hadn't figured out that small towns weren't all that different from cities—people ranged from being blindly set in their ways, to others who were smart, savvy, and knew exactly where they wanted to be.

She should have known it was a mistake dragging Neil to a pizza parlor—it was hardly his speed—but she'd had a sudden longing for something spicy and dripping with cheese.

"No, thanks. How about a large pepperoni, olive and mushroom pizza, with extra cheese?" Neil suggested.

It was almost her idea of the perfect pizza—put onions on top and it *would* be perfect. On the other hand, she didn't want to have onion breath around Neil, so Libby nodded agreement and Sue took off for the kitchen. A friendly argument about Tuck's Italian chicken started immediately, but so did the sound of clanking pots and pans.

"I'm sorry," Libby apologized after a minute. "But I doubt we'd find a place with a wine list around here."

Neil rolled his shoulders as if to work out a kink in his muscles. "This is fine. Actually, if I wasn't driving I'd have a beer."

"If you don't mind, I could drive," she offered.

To her surprise he agreed and ordered some light beer. It probably wouldn't contain enough alcohol to relax him, but she hoped it would take his mind off less pleasant thoughts. She didn't know if the reminder of Neil's father had made him so quiet, but something was responsible.

"Did you think I'd object to a woman behind the wheel?" he asked after a long moment.

"No, but it's your Blazer. Most people don't like someone else driving their car."

"Maybe." He stared at the golden liquid in his glass, turning it this way and that. "Libby, you have to believe I think you're terrific at all this. You're smart and see beyond the surface much better than I can—it's great the way you get swept into seeing what's possible. That's why I wasn't angry this afternoon."

The pink color in her cheeks deepened. "Thank you."

With any other woman Neil would have expected she'd fish for more compliments, but not Libby. In fact, he was realizing she was quite different from the women he'd known, both professionally and socially.

Hell, if she wasn't so damned desirable she'd be the perfect vice president.

Neil took a long swallow of his beer.

He wanted to kiss her, get lost in her sweet scent and warmth and forget the thoughts nagging at the edge of his mind. He should have done it at the duck pond, but good sense had reared its ugly head.

He wouldn't kiss her tonight, either, because it wasn't proper and she might think he was trying to start something.

And the worst of it was, she might be right.

Chapter Nine

Libby sat on the edge of her bed and listened to the shower running in the room next door.

To her relief they'd driven out to the freeway to find a better motel. She didn't mind something simple, or even shabby, but the broken-down motel in Griffith had given her the creeps.

Griffith sat on one of the approaches to Mount Saint Helens. The eruption of the volcano many years ago should have turned it into a prosperous tourist town, but Griffith hadn't reacted quickly enough following the eruption, or else by then the town's people were just too tired and discouraged to make the effort.

Libby flopped backward and stared up at the ceiling. Neil had found a nice place for them to stay, with sterile, impersonal rooms and enormous beds. King-size beds. The kind you ought to be sharing with someone.

Great.

And just who would she share it with?

A vision of Neil filled her head and she growled out loud. She would have sworn he was going to kiss her again, but it hadn't happened and now she was going crazy wondering why. "Why?" was a stupid question. She'd gotten nervous and asked about him being mad, and everything had gone down from there.

It wasn't even that she wanted him to kiss her.

Except she did.

Rolling onto her side, Libby traced the pattern on the bedspread with the tip of her finger. The water was still running next door, and imagining what Neil looked like in the shower was totally distracting.

Women who used the company fitness center said he worked out every night. He ran several miles on the treadmill, then lifted weights for a half hour, followed by twenty minutes on the rowing machine—all wearing a sweatshirt with cutoff sleeves and a pair of shorts that made feminine hearts palpitate wildly.

Something thudded next door and Libby grabbed a pillow, pulling it over her head. It didn't help. A vision of water streaming over powerful muscles rose in front of her eyes.

All at once a tremendous crash in the next room made Libby sit bolt upright.

She dashed outside to Neil's door and pounded on it. "Neil? What happened? Are you all right?"

The sound of muffled cursing ended as the door opened.

Neil.

With a towel wrapped around his lean hips, and the rest of him quite bare.

Libby gulped.

He seemed completely unaware of his near nudity, and she wished she could feel the same. Her entire body was reacting, with tingles racing from her scalp to her toes, and all the way back again.

"Are you…" She stopped, suddenly realizing blood was trickling from his right eyebrow. "You're bleeding."

"It's nothing. I bent over to get the soap and the damned curtain rod fell and hit me. Get in here, you must be freezing out there," Neil said abruptly, turning around.

She must be freezing? She wasn't the one with just a skimpy motel towel covering his wet birthday suit. Shaking her head, Libby stepped inside. "Do you have a first-aid kit?" she asked.

"Can't say that I do."

"I'll get mine, then."

"Did you remember your key?"

Libby groaned. No, she hadn't thought to grab her key, she'd just thought of finding out what had happened to him. Muttering to herself, she went into the bathroom and collected a clean washcloth.

She sucked in a breath when she spun around and found Neil right behind her, just inches away. She couldn't decide if he was every woman's dream, or her nightmare. It was like that milk commercial, where you got a scrumptious cookie to eat, then discovered there was nothing to wash it down with.

"Uh…why don't you sit down on the…uh…"

"The bed?" he asked smoothly.

"Unless you want to sit on the toilet," Libby snapped, hating the way he unnerved her.

"Not really." Neil gave a small hitch to his towel and sauntered into the other room. She glanced at herself in the mirror and made a face, but she frowned when she realized the glass wasn't fogged.

"Did you run out of hot water?" she asked, following him.

"I wouldn't know."

Libby dabbed gently at his eyebrow, trying to see how badly he was cut. Fortunately the bleeding seemed to have stopped, so it wasn't serious. "You were the one in the shower."

"Yeah, but I was using cold water—sort of had to, to get things under control." He said it so silkily she barely noticed, then her cheeks flamed.

"You must have appreciated Sue's T-shirt," she said. "Or rather, you appreciated what was filling it out."

It was a catty thing to say, especially since she'd liked the other woman, but she'd felt undeniably drab by comparison. A blouse and skirt were tame compared to painted on jeans and a two-sizes-too-small T-shirt.

"Actually, I prefer more subtlety. Come here."

One minute Libby was standing, the next she was lying on the bed looking up at Neil.

"I've taken a lot of cold showers lately," he murmured. "*Before* meeting our charming and very married waitress."

His forefinger traced the neckline of her eyelet blouse and she stopped breathing for a minute.

"S-sounds uncomfortable."

"Trust me, the alternative is worse." Neil's hand slipped lower, gliding over her tummy and abdomen in slow, lingering circles, and she bit her lip to keep from purring. The man might be impossible, but he had moments of pure genius.

"I wouldn't have thought you'd need cold showers.

I mean, you've always seemed so much in control,''
Libby said, hardly able to think.

The lovely caresses ended and Neil dropped onto
the mattress next to her, shading his eyes with the
back of his hand. "Control is an illusion. You should
know that by now, with your mother being sick for
so long.''

She sighed, and turned toward him. Her breast
brushed his arm and she wiggled backward in embarrassment.

"Don't," Neil said, putting his hand on her waist.
"That felt nice.''

"That's just because I'm warm and your skin temperature's around fourteen degrees," she muttered.

"Oh, no. Not because of that." He tugged until she
was flush with his body, and though his skin was
undoubtedly chilled, the part of him snuggled against
her hips seemed to be warming up. "You have some
very nice...topography.''

Though she felt herself blushing again, Libby
chuckled. "Is that what you call it?''

"Actually, 'nice' is too lukewarm. It's more like
spectacular topography.''

If it was so spectacular, she wondered why he was
still talking, instead of kissing. Of course, a modern
woman wouldn't wait for him, she'd just jump right
in and...

Putting thought into action, Libby pressed a kiss to
Neil's mouth, and almost instantly began scooting
way.

"Where are you going?''

He caught her close, his lips covering hers with a
demanding force. But the pressure gentled almost instantly, becoming coaxing, seductive, and so hot she

felt flushed all over. Where were her principles? The ones that said she shouldn't be doing anything intimate with a man she didn't like.

But was that still true?

Not about her principles, but about liking him.

Neil's attempts to change since they'd begun working together were no longer so surprising. He'd shown extraordinary compassion to Margie and hadn't crowed once about it, instead avoiding the subject altogether.

"Is this all right?" he breathed between kisses.

"What?"

"This," Neil muttered, giving into temptation and cupping Libby's breast in his hand. Her nipple, firm and taut, burned the center of his palm and his cold shower was nothing but a distant, unpleasant memory.

What had happened to him?

What about his resolution not to start something? What about keeping things friendly and uninvolved? Hell, any hope of that was probably lost the minute he'd seen that silk nightgown she'd claimed was a wedding shower gift. She was such an odd mix of sex and innocence, he couldn't figure her out.

Libby arched upward and his breath went out in a rush. The firm, smooth curves of her breast plumped and he swept his thumb over the hard crown. Blood pooled, hot and urgent at the top of his thighs. He couldn't remember the last time he'd felt so exhilarated, or when it had really mattered who he was holding.

Libby mattered.

She mattered so much it was making him nervous.

Her fingers cupped the back of his neck, encouraging him, and he slid his tongue between her teeth, tasting dark hints of chocolate and coffee, while he waited for her to object. In the past weeks he'd learned that Libby had a passion for lattes—though she insisted on nonfat, decaffeinated, sugar-free concoctions that rightly deserved the moniker of "why bother." But he didn't care. Her own sweet flavor was far more enticing than the finest coffee on the planet.

"Libby…" Whatever he'd intended to say was lost in a groan of pleasure when the inner curve of her foot stroked down the length of his leg and traced a spiral on his ankle.

Where had she learned *that?*

Oh…man, she was something.

"Tell me, just how experienced are you?" he asked between nibbling kisses.

Libby blinked. Wasn't it obvious to Neil she was still a virgin? She'd met some nice men, but no one she'd fallen in love with, and sleeping with a guy just because she liked him wasn't enough reason. That might be too "preacher's daughterish" of her, but that's the way it was.

"Libby?"

"I haven't asked *you* about that," she prevaricated.

"No." Neil lifted his head. He stroked her face and the heightened sensitivity of her nerves sent shivers through her body, followed by the tips of his fingers, down her jaw, to her collar bone. "I suppose it would sound like bragging if I said I've never had any complaints."

"I suppose it would." But she had trouble not smiling, because she was quite certain Neil *didn't* get any complaints. His technique was superb.

Unfortunately, thinking about the women who'd

benefited from that technique was like a splash of icy water, and the urge to smile vanished.

A faint tug on the fabric told her he was unbuttoning the top button of her blouse. The second button went, and then the third. The soft fabric parted enough to expose her bra.

Her eyes closed, rushing warmth replacing the brief chill.

It was a mistake not to put an end to the moment, but she didn't resist when he unfastened the front clasp. One handed. *She* couldn't unhook her own bra with one hand and Neil had done it with three fingers.

It was something she'd think about later, because right now she couldn't think at all.

All at once he put his hands on her waist and rolled her on top of him. "Look at me, Libby," he said urgently.

Her eyes fluttered open and she tried to focus through the rush of her pulse. "W-what?"

"I'll stop whenever you want. Is it…should I stop…now?" he asked, sounding like he really hoped the answer was *no*.

Stopping was the last thing on her mind. Feeling wanton and out-of-control, Libby shook her head and rubbed herself over him. The movement freed one of her breasts and the light abrasion of her nipple across his bare chest sent heat straight to the base of her stomach.

She heard a muttered curse, or maybe a prayer, and Neil pulled her mouth down to his.

Unlike his gentle exploring before, his tongue thrust boldly, claiming his territory with predatory ease. Neil might have smoothed some of his rough edges recently, but he was still the maverick conqueror who got whatever he wanted.

But that was all right, because she felt free to explore his chest and shoulders in ways she'd never touched a man, and the yearning deep inside her abdomen became an urgent, aching void that had to be filled. He was amazing. Hard and fit, with smooth skin except for the narrow wedge of dark hair between his pectoral muscles.

"Neil, you...um..."

Her words were lost when he brushed the sides of her breasts. Bracing herself on his chest, Libby lifted up, giving him full access. At the sensation of hard fingers tugging and rolling her nipples, Libby moaned. Whether for good or ill, the sound brought her to her senses.

This was going way too fast, and way too far.

Though her instincts said to rip the damp towel from Neil's hips and demand he settle the need in her body, she shook her head instead, trying to clear it.

"Neil, stop."

Stop?

Neil wanted to ask if she was insane, yet at the same time he knew she was right. A woman had the right to say no, any time, any place. And this wasn't the right time or place to make love to her, anyway.

Chest heaving, he locked his hands behind the back of his neck to avoid grabbing Libby back. But instead of leaving, she curled up next to him and he saw tears glinting on her lashes.

"Libby, what's wrong?"

"Nothing."

Yeah, he bought that.

"Talk to me. That's the only way the top of my head isn't going to blow off."

A ghost of a smile tugged at her lips and he wanted to kiss her all over again. "I was just thinking how safe I feel right now," she admitted.

He frowned. A hotel room with a naked man was the last place she should feel safe. "Come again?"

She shrugged and swept her hair back over her shoulder.

Her hair.

Hell, he'd barely had a chance to slide his fingers into that heavy length of silk. How could he have neglected it? He was slipping, missing his opportunities. Of course, he'd had other temptations, like the taut weight of her breasts. Even now her creamy curves were revealed through folds of her blouse, the raspberry pink of a nipple was framed by the white eyelet fabric.

With an effort, Neil focused on Libby's face. "I'm not the least bit safe," he managed to say.

"Yes, you are. I can't explain it." She smoothed her finger over the hair on his chest. "I knew you'd stop. It never crossed my mind that you wouldn't."

Neil grabbed one of the king-size pillows from under the bedspread and eased it beneath Libby's head on one end, and put his own head on the other. Part of him was aching more than ever before, yet he also felt terrific. Whatever his flaws might be, knowing this particular woman trusted him seemed more important than a thousand business deals.

"Does this hurt?" Libby asked, the tip of her finger skimming the spot where the shower rod had struck him. "I don't think you had enough to drink at dinner to kill the pain."

"One light beer?" Neil's injured eyebrow shot upward. "Not hardly. Besides, it was just a glancing blow. I've survived worse, like getting mugged in New York."

"Mugged?"

"Just a couple of kids," he said dismissively. "One wasn't a bad fighter, but the other had a glass jaw."

Was that where he'd gotten the tiny scar under his eyebrow? Libby had never noticed it, but she'd never been lying next to him before, talking after very nearly making love. Her body was reminding her just *how* close they'd come, mostly through shivers of frustration. It was so strange feeling peaceful and chaotic, all at the same time.

"And one of those 'kids' could have had a gun," she said sharply, yet her words wavered slightly. "Don't do that again, just give them what they want. A few credit cards and a watch aren't worth your life. I don't care if it is a Rolex."

"Worried about me?"

Neil kept a tender smile from his face, knowing Libby wouldn't understand. It wouldn't occur to her to bolster his ego by telling him he was wonderful for being stupid enough to face down two punks in Central Park. She cared too much about people and had too much sense.

"Of course I'm worried. It would upset Kane if something happened to you."

Her acerbic tone didn't fool him. Libby had a soft heart that he'd learned to appreciate in a way he could never have imagined. Sometimes when he looked at the way he'd always been, mowing through people's feelings, he was disgusted with himself.

"Sorry I got moody earlier," he whispered.

"You were thinking about…" She hesitated.

"About my dad." Neil brushed a lock of hair from her forehead. "I've been thinking about him a lot lately. I'm not sure why, except maybe it's wanting to know what he'd think of my life, of what I've done with my career."

If he'd think it's enough.

"I'm sure he'd be proud of you."

Maybe.

"My dad used to make furniture—great, handcrafted pieces," Neil said. "He loved it, but it didn't pay much. To support the family he got a job with a logging company, and worked weekends as a handyman. So it was because of *us* he died in the forest, doing something he didn't like."

Libby kissed the corner of his mouth, and he cleared his throat. What was it about her that turned him inside out? And why had it taken so long to value the sweet, tender possibilities of a woman like Libby?

"Do you think he resented his choice?" she asked.

The question surprised Neil, and his forehead creased as he thought about it. Keenan O'Rourke had rarely taken a day—or even an hour—off from supporting his family; his "code" had insisted he do what was necessary. *Had* his father resented choosing the family over work that fulfilled him?

Never, son.

Neil's eyes widened as his dad's voice echoed in his mind. It was as if Keenan was in the room, speaking not just to his ears, but to his heart.

"No," he said slowly. "Dad wouldn't have resented it. He had an unbreakable code about being a man and how to make your way in the world. Regretting his choices wasn't part of that code.''

"What do you remember most about him?"

"His smile," Neil murmured, his own lips curving. "Dad's smile made you feel as if nothing could go wrong. When I was a kid I thought he was a superhero in disguise—that they'd somehow gotten it wrong in the comic books.''

Libby tucked her arms in front of her, discreetly gathering the edges of her blouse together. At first she hadn't been conscious of her bare skin, bra and blouse askew from Neil's caresses, but no longer. Why couldn't she be like Neil? He seemed completely comfortable with just a towel pulled carelessly over his hips.

"You used to read comic books?'' she asked.

"Not after I decided they were all wrong.''

"How old was that?''

"Seven. I was almost seventeen when Dad was killed, so I got another ten years of memories before the worst happened. I guess I'm lucky. My youngest sister was so young at the time she barely remembers him.''

"That Kathleen, right?'' Libby murmured and he nodded.

She liked Kathleen. Actually, she liked all of the O'Rourkes except for Neil, and he was starting to grow on her.

A wry honesty made Libby roll her eyes. Neil was *more* than growing on her, he was monopolizing her thoughts. Worse, he was creeping into her heart no matter how hard she fought it. She couldn't even wear that silly indulgent nightgown she'd purchased, because she couldn't sleep for wondering if he'd approve of the way she looked in it. She ought to have been more practical and saved her money.

Neil wasn't looking for a fairy princess to share his castle. Which was a really dumb thought, because she didn't believe in fairy-tale princes. Except…Neil was better than a prince. He was real and warm and exciting, and she was getting too involved for her own good.

"I should go down to the office and get a replacement key," she said reluctantly, hating to disturb the moment.

"I'll get dressed and go with you."

"That's all right. I can't get into trouble between here and the office."

"No."

The adamant look on Neil's face told her it wouldn't do any good to argue. She was tempted to tease him about being old-fashioned in his attitude toward women, but he'd probably take it too seriously.

"Then I'll close my eyes."

She closed them, and heard him chuckle. "I think I'll take care of you first."

Libby jumped when his fingers began fastening the hooks and buttons he'd unfastened earlier.

"Are you peeking?" she asked as he took his time drawing the bra over her breasts, slipping every now and then to caress her skin. Her heart began pounding again so hard she figured he could see it practically jumping from her chest.

"Of course I'm peeking. I'm a guy, we're genetically programmed to look whenever possible. You said it yourself, men just think about sex."

She winced.

"Uh…about that, I really ought to apo—''

Neil put his palm over her mouth and she looked into his gray eyes smiling down at her. How could she have ever thought they were cold?

"I have an idea," he said. "Let's forget about the things we said before we got better acquainted. As I recall I said a few things that I'd rather you didn't remember."

Libby bobbed her head and couldn't resist kissing the palm nestled against her mouth. Neil's breath came out harshly.

"Lady, I can't remember the last time I felt this way," he muttered. "Go ahead and peek all you like."

He swung away from the bed, unhitching the towel from around his hips. It landed in an untidy heap on the floor, and Libby openly watched as he grabbed his clothes. It was silly to think of a modern man like Neil in terms of Greek statues, but the line and power of his body did remind her of a classical sculpture. Of course, she doubted a sculpture had ever depicted such an aroused male.

"You *are* peeking," Neil said, sounding surprised when he turned around.

"By invitation."

"I didn't think virgins looked."

"What makes you think virgins don't care about looking?" she asked, still unwilling to admit the truth.

Neil just shrugged. He finished buckling his belt buckle, and she sighed, thinking he was even more scrumptious in jeans and a pullover sweater than his designer suits.

"What makes you think virgins don't think about sex?" she continued. "Or that they don't lie awake sometimes at night and wish there was a man in their bed, instead of a cat? And I don't mean for cuddling and warmth, but for outrageous sex? What makes you think women are like Sleeping Beauty, needing to be awakened by a man before they feel like you do?''

Dear heaven. Neil thought he was going to drop dead of a heart attack. He'd never imagined a virgin felt that way, and the fact it was Libby saying those things made him want to howl.

He opened his mouth, then closed it again when she shook her head.

''I'm sorry,'' she said. ''I'm just nervous.''

''*You're* nervous?'' he croaked.

''Yes. I don't know how you really feel about me…uh…being a…'' Her voice trailed, but instead of flushing pink with embarrassment, her skin turned pale.

Tension flew out of him, replaced by understanding. He could say they should forget the things they'd said to one another, but it didn't change the fact that he'd once been contemptuous of her innocence.

''I've grown up since the day we met,'' Neil said quietly. ''Boys say a lot of things when they're trying to get a girl into bed, or when their pride is wounded. Foolish things they're ashamed of later. A grown man doesn't try to manipulate a woman into giving him something she doesn't want to give, and he respects the choices she makes. It's that simple.''

Libby straightened her skirt without looking at him, then fingered the gold chain around her neck. She was still pale, and he ached with the need to make her understand.

He crouched next to her and lifted her chin. ''When my brother said you had qualities I needed, I was angry. But it wasn't because of you, it was my pride getting in the way again, not wanting to admit I couldn't go it alone. But Kane was right. I'm a better person because of you, Libby, so how could I think you're anything but wonderful?''

Libby swallowed. Neil's eyes blazed with sincerity, and she blinked away a tear.

Her heart and mind and body were so stirred up she could barely think, but she believed him.

Chapter Ten

"Come on." Neil grabbed Libby's hand and pulled her to her feet. "We'd better get a duplicate key for your room before I forget I'm all grown up now, and try to get you back in bed using all the sneaky adolescent tricks at my disposal."

Libby's chin lifted with a hint of her normal stubbornness. "Those tricks didn't work for you before, what makes you think they'd work now?"

"Hey, that's right. Guess you were smarter than me, even eleven years ago."

He deliberately kept his tone light and teasing, hoping he'd never see that somber expression on Libby's face again. It was bound to happen, but he'd rather cut off his right arm than be the one to put it there.

He pulled his coat around her shoulders before they went outside, though she didn't seem to get cold the way most people did. Libby accepted the gesture with a smile.

The desk clerk nodded as they walked in. "How can I help you?" he asked genially.

"Miss Dumont needs a duplicate key to her room," Neil explained. "She's locked out."

"Oh, well, that happens."

The man chuckled and popped a plastic key into the machine to electronically code it. Calling something the size and feel of a credit card a "key" seemed odd, but that was the modern world. They wouldn't have anything like that in their bed and breakfast inns. Instead, they'd have real keys and locks that offered the feel of earlier days.

Libby's enthusiasm was contagious. His imagination was filled with the possibilities of creating gracious and elegant places for people to enjoy. They could do so much with a house like the one in Griffith or the other gems they'd found, especially with a partner like Libby.

The desk clerk took a call, and while they were waiting, Libby wandered over to the rack holding advertisements for various Washington state attractions. He wondered if she was envisioning flyers for the bed-and-breakfast inns they were creating. She might even be designing them in her head.

"Here you go," said the clerk when he'd hung up the receiver. "Just like a little lady to forget her key." He chortled, obviously thinking he'd said something witty and wise.

From the corner of his eye Neil saw Libby looked annoyed, but he doubted she'd say anything about the "little lady" remark, she was too polite.

He, on the other hand, was known for being rude, arrogant and pushy, and he'd be damned if he let someone belittle Libby.

"Miss Dumont forgot her key out of concern for me," he said icily. "The shower rod fell off the bathroom wall and hit me on the face. The noise alarmed her and she rushed to help. So make an effort not to say something more stupid than you have to, all right?"

The other man shrank backward. "Er...I didn't mean... The motel will...that is, do you need medical attention?" he stuttered.

"No, but you're lucky I'm not planning to sue for every penny this place is worth. Now I suggest you apologize to Miss Dumont for your chauvinistic remark."

"That isn't necessary," Libby assured hastily.

"Yes it *is.*"

The clerk cleared his throat. "I'm quite sorry, miss. I never meant to offend you. And there won't be any charge for the night, of course. For either of you."

Neil grabbed the plastic key and held the door for Libby, who looked torn between wanting to leave, and wanting to soothe the clerk's ruffled feathers. She finally gave him a kind smile, then ducked through the door.

"That was very gallant, but I didn't need you to defend me," she said as they climbed the stairs.

"You're too nice to say anything. Jeez, is that the kind of crap women have to put up with?"

Libby put her hand over her mouth to hide a grin. She'd never known a man willing to go to war for her over something so trivial as an annoying "little lady" remark.

"Comparatively, it wasn't so bad," she murmured. "The male half of my own family can be far worse than that, though they don't have a clue what they're saying most of the time. They think they're modern, progressive guys, but they really belong in the dark ages when it comes to their attitudes.''

''So you just grit your teeth and resist unmasking their fantasy self-image,'' Neil guessed.

''Most of the time.''

They reached their rooms and he handed her the plastic card key. ''You're too nice for your own good. Next time nail 'em for saying something stupid.''

''I'll think about it.''

''Okay. Wait a minute, let me check your room and make sure it's all right,'' he said, taking the key back again.

''I'm sure it's fine.''

Neil ignored her, looking into the bathroom and under the bed, and even checking the windows to be certain they were still fastened. But when he paused at the door to inspect the locks he smiled sheepishly.

''I suppose this makes me as big a hypocrite as the men in your family.''

Her throat was so tight it was hard to talk. Who could have imagined Neil O'Rourke acting like that…endearing and charming, and so lovable her heart was having a hard time not falling head over heels?

''I'll let you in on a secret,'' she said when she'd managed to regain her composure. ''Deep down a lot of modern women really *do* want a knight in shining armor, but they also want the knight to respect their abilities and understand they can handle things alone. We don't like explaining because it's contradictory and confusing and guys might get the wrong idea. So I'm not sure who's the hypocrite, or if it's just part of being human.''

"Which really means I'm damned if I do, and damned if I don't?" he asked with a grin.

"Something like that."

"You're right, it is confusing." Neil tossed the key on the bed. "I think I'll just follow my dad's code of honor and resign myself to being called a sexist jerk for it."

"You aren't a jerk."

"But I'm a sexist?"

"No." Libby smiled. "Only I think you're more like small town people than you want to admit."

"Small town, huh?" Neil chuckled. "I've been called worse."

In Neil O'Rourke's lexicon being "small town" was probably an insult, but she hadn't meant it that way. "It's a compliment. No matter what you believe, the biggest difference between country folks and city dwellers is where they want to live."

"I'm not so sure of that, but if everyone in small towns was like you, Libby, I think I could spend the rest of my life in Endicott as a happy man." He gave her a swift kiss and stepped outside. "I'll see you in the morning."

Libby touched her tingling lips as she shut the door and leaned against it, breathing so hard her head spun. Keeping her perspective was hard, particularly with Neil confounding her on so many fronts.

She slid down until she was sitting on the ground and didn't have so far to fall if she kept hyperventilating.

Okay, Neil was turning into a nice guy. It could happen to anybody. Nobody was all bad and he'd had the right influences from childhood—great mom, terrific dad, and plenty of brothers and sisters, all raised with good, solid values.

But there was his commitment problem to consider.

Nothing he'd said suggested a change in attitude about a wife and kids. His girlfriends never lasted, and he wasn't exactly the home and hearth sort of guy. He liked eating in fine restaurants, traveling, the theater, nightlife, and high-rise apartments. Seattle was a gorgeous city, but it was still a city and she liked her lakeside home where foxes and deer came to drink at the water's edge every morning.

Neil seemed to enjoy kissing her, but that didn't mean much. Sex for men usually meant something different than it did for women, even her dear, absentminded father admitted that.

Neil might desire her, but it was only for the moment and wouldn't last.

More than anything, Libby wanted to cry, but she wouldn't give in to the weakness. She was the one the family depended on, the one they relied on when something went wrong. Everyone called her a mother hen, and men like Neil didn't want mother hens for girlfriends *or* wives. But that was okay, because she liked taking care of her family and being needed.

She had to be practical.

Realistic.

And somehow get through the next two days of their scouting trip without doing something unbelievably foolish—like falling in love with Neil.

The next morning Neil woke before dawn and stretched, inordinately pleased with life. There was a slight ache over his right eye from the shower curtain rod, but other than that he felt great.

Which was really odd because he'd expected to be tense as hell after spending a chaste night without Libby in his bed.

There was only one way to get her into his bed, and that was to marry her.

The idea of marriage no longer sent cold chills down his spine, but it was a lot to think about. Most importantly, he had to face the fact he wasn't ideal husband material for a sweetheart like Libby.

It was an ego deflating concept, and his mood sobered as he shaved and got dressed. In college when he'd thought he was in love and asked the girl to marry him, she'd turned him down because he wasn't rich and well-connected. Those things wouldn't count to Libby.

In fact, he might not have a single quality she was looking for in a husband, and that possibility *did* send cold chills down his spine.

Hell.

Neil changed from his jeans to a pair of sweats. The motel was located on a long frontage road, and he needed to work off his sudden uneasiness.

Wasn't that the limit?

You spend an entire life figuring on one thing, then start to change your mind and realize you might have screwed up simply because you didn't change gears fast enough.

Outside the air was cold and crisp, with the first rime of frost on the ground. He stretched for a couple of minutes, then took off down the dimly lit road.

"I've been thinking," Libby said over breakfast.

Well, *she* called what she was eating breakfast, but Neil preferred something more substantial in the morning than a bowl of fruit and a chocolate-flavored latte.

"About what?" he said, digging into his steak and fried eggs. One thing he liked about country restaurants was the food they served in the morning. Especially after running several miles on an empty stomach.

"We shouldn't…that is, we have to remember we're professionals with a job to do. Kane doesn't have a policy against fraternizing amongst employees, but getting involved usually creates more problems than it's worth."

Criminy.

His juicy steak suddenly tasted like shoe leather.

"I'm sure you agree," Libby said. "Not that we're actually involved, or anything," she added.

"No, of course not."

She pushed her fork around the fruit in her bowl. "And we both agreed we didn't want to be involved, right in the beginning. You said yourself that you weren't interested in starting anything."

Personally, Neil thought he'd said some stupid things, and that had to be the stupidest.

Not want to start something?

Of course he'd wanted to start something. He was a guy, and Libby was stacked. She had a smile like warm sunshine, and he'd been attracted to her for eleven years. He'd done his best to pretend she didn't exist since they were so obviously incompatible, but that hadn't changed his basic, gut-level response on the rare occasions they'd run into each other.

"Neil?" Libby prompted.

"Yeah, go on."

Confusion clouded her green eyes, but he was trying to think of something to say that wouldn't get his face slapped, or the door permanently slammed on him before he figured out what he really wanted. For now it was probably safer if she kept talking.

"There isn't a lot more to say. I enjoyed last night, but we shouldn't let it happen again."

Oh, this wasn't good.

"Nothing happened. Not really."

"I suppose that's true from your point of view," Libby said tartly and he winced.

Fine.

They could back off from one another while they were sorting stuff out. It wasn't the end of the world and it would give him time to regroup. Except it *might* be the end of the world, and he just didn't have the good sense to see it. Still, considering their positions, he couldn't push without looking like he was taking advantage.

"Okay."

She looked at him suspiciously. "Okay, what?"

"Okay. We'll do what you want."

Libby nodded, feeling miserable all over again. Neil hadn't put up much of a fight; he'd mostly listened and then agreed. She ought to be happy, *thrilled,* instead she wanted to kick him. *Again.*

Almost as if sensing her thoughts, Neil shifted his legs away from her. "I like this restaurant," he said, digging into his steak again.

She pushed her fruit aside, giving up the pretense of eating. Even her latte didn't taste good, and she happened to know they used SBC—Seattle's Best Coffee—beans, which was her very favorite coffee company.

"Do you eat like that every morning?" Libby

asked, shuddering at the thought of so much heavy protein hitting her tummy and sitting there all day.

"Only on special occasions."

Swell.

She wondered if their breakup—after not really being involved in the first place—could be considered a special occasion. Her only consolation was knowing he'd ordered his breakfast before she'd suggested they refrain from a repeat of last night's kiss. On the other hand, she might have just beaten him to it.

She pushed her nonfat chocolate latte in the same direction as the fruit.

Things were bad when you didn't even want chocolate.

At the end of their third day on the road Libby had convinced herself that everything was for the best. She and Neil had regained the friendly camaraderie they'd been building, and had discussed the future of their division inside and out. They had four new properties for the bed-and-breakfast line, and were ready to begin contracting for restoration work.

Really.

It was all for the best.

Maybe she could even start to concentrate on Christmas. It was close to the holidays, and though she'd helped decorate the church and her parents' house, she hadn't put up even a wreath or silver bell on her own, or shopped for a single gift. She would do it on Saturday, if only to prove to herself that her life could go on despite her inner turmoil.

Stretching tiredly, Libby glanced into the backseat to see how Bilbo was doing in his cat carrier. Neil had insisted on driving to Endicott to get him, though she'd said she was going up over the weekend.

"Is he okay?"

"He's fine." She smiled wryly. "Bilbo takes things in his stride. Right now he's sound asleep with his face smooshed up against the carrier door."

"I've never seen such a big feline." Neil shook his head. "Are you certain he doesn't have a little tiger blood in his veins?"

"Just pure Maine Coon. They can weigh over thirty pounds. Look, you really don't have to take me to my house," Libby said abruptly. "I need my car, anyway, to get to work tomorrow."

"We've been over this. I'll send the limo out in the morning. It doesn't make sense for you to drive into Seattle, and back out again. It'd be dark before you got there. Now, where do I turn?"

Libby gave up. Knowing Neil, he intended to inspect the house to be sure nobody had broken in during her absence—never mind she got home after dark most winter evenings, he was going to ensure her safety. She would have enjoyed the gallantry more if he had personal reasons for being concerned about her, which just went to show she was being irrational.

"Turn at the gas station," she muttered.

He followed her instructions, winding through the hills until they drove through the thick band of evergreen forest that surrounded her property.

"Whoa, this is nice," he said.

"Probably too quiet for you."

"You never know." Neil helped Libby down and lifted the enormous cat carrier from the back seat. "I'll get your luggage in a minute."

"Going to check the house out?"

"Yeah, but only because I'm a man and can't help myself."

She laughed and handed him the key. He noted the sturdy locks on the door and the placement of good lighting around the property with approval.

Libby's home surprised him, though it shouldn't have. It was a modern, two-story log house. The interior was open and airy, with large windows that revealed a small, but picturesque natural lake beyond the broad deck. She obviously didn't have a fondness for clutter and knickknacks, preferring instead a scattering of deep, rich blues and greens that complimented the hardwood floors and beamed ceiling.

It was tranquil, like Libby.

A celebration of the senses. He would never underestimate her again.

"Is it all clear?" she called from the doorway.

"Just a minute." Still absorbing the peace he felt from every corner, Neil quickly inspected the spacious rooms, though he couldn't help lingering in her upstairs bedroom.

Desire hit him like a sledgehammer at the sight of a queen-size bed covered by a rich green comforter and piled with pillows. Coiled rag rugs of blue and green sat jewel-like on the oak floor, seeming an extension of the world of water and evergreen outside, revealed by a bank of south-facing windows.

If that wasn't enough, the bathroom was a sensual delight, with a whirlpool tub that sat in a corner of glass fire brick walls, masses of leafy plants, and an overhead skylight.

He wanted Libby.

He wanted her in that bed, for hours and hours.

After that they'd check out the tub for a while. It

would be like making love in a jungle. Then they'd go back to bed.

"Neil?"

"I'll be down in a minute."

He put his hand on the doorframe and practiced his deep breathing. Libby was the one who'd put up the Don't Touch signs, so he was obligated to respect her wishes. But it was driving him crazy.

By the time he got downstairs Libby had obviously gotten tired of waiting for him. Bilbo was stretched out on the couch and she was carrying her suitcase in from the Blazer.

"Hey, I said I'd get that," Neil said, grabbing it away. "You want this in your bedroom?"

"Yes, thank you. It's at the top—"

"Of the stairs. I know."

Libby sighed as she stroked Bilbo's broad head and heard his purr rumble loudly in the stillness. It was better being friendly with Neil, instead of romantic.

Really.

And if she kept telling herself that, she might actually start to believe it.

Chapter Eleven

"You're a mess."

Neil scowled up at his brother from the chaise lounge in his mother's backyard. "Thanks, Kane, I didn't know that." He closed his eyes and pretended to sleep, which was quite a feat since it was forty degrees outside and he was only wearing a light jacket.

At least it wasn't raining.

"Mom wants to know if you're spending the afternoon out here, or plan to eat dinner with the rest of us," Kane murmured.

"Give me a break, I haven't been sleeping lately."

"Dare I ask why?"

"Why the hell not? Everyone else has been asking."

"So?"

"So I can't sleep, that's all." Neil closed his eyes again, but all he could see was Libby's face, which was exactly *why* he couldn't sleep. He hadn't thought about her that much—only every five minutes or so, and he wasn't any closer to making a decision.

Maybe because he was afraid it was too late for a decision.

Kane prodded his foot. "Talk to me. I'm sure there's a solution."

"That's because you don't know the problem." Neil lifted one eyelid. "Even if it's all your fault."

His brother sat on a nearby lawn chair and smiled quizzically. "How do you figure that?"

"You made Libby Dumont my vice president."

"So?"

"So she's like this forbidden candy that you can't stop thinking about. Then you get a little taste, and that isn't nearly enough, so you want more, only you're not sure how much. And then the candy says take a hike, and you have to respect that because it turns out you've got a code of honor, even if you haven't thought about it in a long time."

Kane whistled. "Libby told you to take a hike?"

"Not exactly, but if I'd had any sense I would have changed the subject instead of chowing down on steak and eggs."

"Why didn't you change the subject?"

"I thought I'd get into more trouble by talking."

"This is interesting. You want to have an affair with Libby Dumont."

"I didn't say an affair," Neil snapped, annoyed. Jeez, didn't Kane know Libby any better than that? She'd been his executive assistant for years before promoting her. "You aren't listening."

Kane lifted an eyebrow. "I'm listening, you just aren't being concise. Which I must say is really out of character for you."

Sheesh.

Neil swung his legs to the ground and sat up; he should have known better than to come to the weekly family dinner. The O'Rourkes were bloodhounds when it came to nosing into each other's business—all from the best of intentions, of course, but still a pain.

He'd hardly gotten a minute of sleep since leaving Libby's house last Thursday afternoon. Some of it was from sexual frustration, but the rest was from playing things over and over in his head and trying to figure out if things had really gone wrong, and what to do about it.

They'd kissed, then laughed together. That was usually a good sign. She'd remembered what a jerk he'd been a long time ago, but sassy mouth or not, Libby wasn't the type to hold a grudge. Then she'd said they shouldn't have any repeats of them kissing. He should have listened closer to that part, then he wouldn't be so bugged about it now and wondering how serious she'd been.

"I will deal with this on my own," he said, fumbling in his pockets for his car keys.

"You seem to be screwing this up on your own, too."

It was the truth, and Neil rubbed his forehead. "Like I didn't already know that. Libby is so amazing. I had no idea what she was really like. She's that one-of-a-kind woman you didn't think existed."

He glanced at Kane and saw him smile. It wasn't an irritating sort of smile; it was the one he wore when he was thinking about Beth.

"You knew this would happen, didn't you?" Neil asked, resigned. "You knew Libby would get to me."

"I wondered."

"You know, my life was just fine without your interference. I had everything sorted out and going the way I wanted. Now it's all gone to hell."

Kane clasped his shoulders. "If your life was so great before, then Libby wouldn't have put you in a tailspin. Tell me, have you started hearing Dad yet?"

Neil froze. He'd heard Keenan O'Rourke's voice several times since Libby had asked if his father ever regretted his choices. It was weird and reassuring at the same time. "How do you know about that?"

"Because it happened to me, and to Patrick when he was courting Maddie. It makes sense. Nothing was more important to Dad than Mother and the family, so it figures he'd find a way to reach us when we're facing the most important decision of our lives."

"And maybe it's just our imaginations."

His brother shook his head. "You know what Mom says—heaven gives us what we need. I think Libby is what you need, and you just have to accept the gift. Now let's go eat dinner before it gets cold."

"I'll be there in a minute."

But Neil stayed much longer than a minute, thinking about Libby and the way she smiled, and how it felt when she was tucked in his arms. Like he was on top of the world.

He rubbed his face hard, trying to clear his tired mind. Exactly how much of a brush-off had she given him? Was it her pride, or worry that he wasn't the sort of man she wanted to be involved with? He couldn't seem like a great husband prospect after the cutting things he'd always said about marriage and children.

"When you mess up, you do it good," Neil muttered. He'd been so determined to make sure the women he became involved with knew the score, he'd never considered what would happen if he changed his mind. On top of everything else, he hadn't said anything to Libby about the future, though he was sure he'd said she was wonderful.

Of course, she might have taken that to mean wonderful at her job. It was true, but she was also just plain wonderful.

With a deep sigh he finally followed his brother into the house. It wasn't going to be easy showing Libby he'd changed, but he'd do whatever it took, because he didn't think he could live the rest of his life without her.

"What do you mean, Neil won't be coming in?" Libby stared at Margie as if she'd said the boss had sprouted wings and flown to the moon.

"He called and said he wouldn't be in the office for a few days. He told me you'd handle everything and to go ahead with whatever contracts are ready. Will you certify my time?"

Libby signed Margie's time sheet and sank into her chair in disbelief. Neil hadn't said anything about taking a few days off on Friday. Instead of sending a limousine he'd picked her up himself, and they'd had a pleasant, totally *non*personal conversation on the way into Seattle, then worked late on some ideas she'd had for a line of clothing stores.

He'd seemed distracted, but nothing serious.

Maybe he was finally getting himself a life. Yet the idea he was getting a life without her was much less pleasant than she might have once thought... especially since he'd escorted a beautiful neurosurgeon to a charity banquet on Saturday evening. A neuro-surgeon who was the precise image of the women he usually dated—tall, cool blondes with designer clothes and lovely composed faces.

"I don't care," she muttered, angry she'd even noticed the newspaper article that talked about the event.

A lot of people had attended that dinner. They were raising money for a new children's wing at the hospital, so it was an important charity. Apparently Neil donated consulting services to the board of directors and was considered responsible for pulling them out of the red. Knowing he was interested in philanthropic concerns was nice to discover, she hadn't heard about it before.

Still…

Libby pulled out the article she'd clipped and stared at it. Neil couldn't be seriously dating another woman. He wouldn't kiss *her* like that, at the same time he was seeing someone else in a not-so-casual way.

"I am completely losing it," she announced to the silent office. "I don't care if he dates a hundred women."

It was a hollow declaration, particularly since she did care.

Why did it feel like everything was falling apart all of a sudden? Over the weekend her parents had refused to take any more money, saying she'd done enough and it was time to live her own life. She *was* living her own life, and she liked being needed. Then she'd seen that article about the hospital gala, and she'd kicked herself for saying anything at all to Neil. She could have just waited to see what would happen, but no, she had to save her pride by being the one to put an end to something that probably existed mostly in her imagination.

Libby stared at her day planner and realized it all looked boring without Neil.

She pushed the planner to one side as Margie walked in, a cheerful bounce to her step. "I'm having lunch at the deli if you want me to get you something," she offered.

"Thanks. I'll treat us both. Order me a Greek salad," Libby said, pulling a twenty from her purse.

Margie smiled her thanks and leaned over to take the twenty, then wrinkled her nose as she spotted the newspaper article on the corner of the desk. "Poor Neil, he wanted out of that charity dinner so bad."

"Oh?" Libby asked, trying to sound casual.

"Yeah, you should have heard him grumbling about it on Friday. But I guess he and Dr. Dailey were co-hosts of the dinner, and he didn't feel he could let her do it alone."

A ridiculous relief swept through Libby. Of course Neil wouldn't let someone down that he'd promised to help.

"I'm sure Dr. Dailey appreciated it."

Margie giggled. "She sent a huge bouquet of flowers to him this morning. I told Neil about it when he called and he said to dump them in the trash. But they're too pretty, so I'm taking them home. I'll be back later with your salad."

Libby took a deep breath and crumpled the clipping into a ball, then tossed it in the waste can.

She only wished she could take care of her aching heart as quickly.

For the next few days Libby juggled negotiations with architects and local contractors, recruiting various employees to handle aspects of the work. On Wednesday morning she drove up to Endicott to review the floor plans of Huckleberry House with a potential architect, and nearly choked when she saw Neil's silver Blazer pull onto the street by the Endicott café.

Curiosity getting the better of her, Libby followed Neil to the house out on Tindale Road. He got out and shook hands with Barton Masterfield, the local contractor she'd talked with about doing work on the Huckleberry House.

This wasn't the property they were buying.

Getting out, she shut her car door with more vigor than necessary, and both Barton and Neil looked at her.

"Hey, Barton," she said, forcing a smile. He'd married one of her old classmates and moved to Endicott to please his wife. The marriage hadn't lasted, but he'd stayed, anyway.

"Libby, what are you doing here?" Neil asked.

"I'm going to make notes on Huckleberry House, and review the floor plan with an architect. I understood you were taking a few days off. What are *you* doing here?"

Barton and Neil exchanged glances, then Barton went inside with visible haste.

"I've decided to buy this house for myself."

"You…what?"

The disbelief on Libby's face wasn't a good sign, but Neil plastered a smile on his mouth. "It's a great weekend retreat. Cross-country skiing is supposed to be excellent up here, and since I liked the house and it's in good shape, I went ahead."

"But you don't like small towns."

"Endicott is growing on me. Besides, there's a terrific view of Mount Rainier from the master bedroom window, and lots of room for kids and visitors and stuff."

"Kids?"

"I'm thinking of it as a family retreat."

Her expression was unreadable, and he had an urge to loosen his collar. For a woman who usually didn't hide her feelings, he was having trouble knowing what to think. He had to be careful; she might have meant what she said about them not being together. He'd do his best to change her mind, of course, but it would be difficult.

"And it's a good investment," he added.

Boy, is that lame, he thought, disgusted with himself. He didn't care if he threw his money down a rat hole if it made Libby happy. Good investing didn't enter into his decision, the only time it *would* was if it meant taking care of his family.

"I see." She looked at her watch and gave her suit jacket a small tug. "I have to go, the architect is meeting me at Huckleberry House in a few minutes."

"I'll go with you."

Libby nodded and he followed her car to the other house. She seemed to be retreating from him, and he wished he'd gone into the office instead of making plans for the house. But he'd hoped it would show her that he wanted more than just work, that he had changed and was thinking about a family. It would take some doing—when he thought of the ridiculous things he'd always said about marriage and children, he had the urge to crawl under the nearest rock.

But he *had* changed and the house was his way of

showing it. Considering how often she visited her parents, it was a good idea for them to have a place in Endicott. Someplace they could be private, but still see the family whenever they wanted.

He'd made other plans, too, but right now didn't seem to be a good time to discuss them.

The architect turned out to be a bubbling, energetic woman in her fifties, wearing wire-rimmed glasses and a pin shaped like a teapot on her lapel. She greeted Libby with a broad smile and handshake, and offered a more restrained greeting to Neil.

"Neil, this is Joyce Nakama. She's specializes in restoration architecture."

"I'd better get busy." Joyce gave him a terse nod, then disappeared into the house, tape measure in one hand and notepad in the other.

"What have you been telling her about me?" he asked.

"Nothing. Your reputation precedes you."

"People can change. Don't you think I've changed?"

Libby gave him a brooding look. She seemed tense and there were faint dark circles beneath her eyes, but she was pure honey to look at. He'd missed her so much, even though it had only been a few days. No wonder Kane rushed home every night to be with Beth if it was anything like the way he felt about Libby.

"I know you don't like me to bring it up, but you've been awfully nice to Margie. She's much less stressed," Libby murmured. "And you've encouraged Duncan. He's really relaxed around you now."

Neil cleared his throat uncomfortably. Originally he'd planned those things with Margie and Dunk Anderson to prove something to himself and to Libby. But people's lives were too important to use that way, it was one of the things she'd taught him.

"I'm the one who benefited," he said. "Margie's a great secretary, and Dunk is funny as hell when he isn't breaking stuff. Did you know he does a standup routine mimicking Kane and me? It's a riot."

"I…yes, I know. You don't mind?"

"He doesn't mean any harm, and people need to laugh. Why should I mind?"

Libby's tummy wobbled. Why couldn't Neil have stayed obnoxious? It was hard not to love someone who was smart and thoughtful and could laugh at himself.

The architect came trotting down the stairs and Libby turned around, grateful for the interruption. "What do you think?"

"I love this house," Joyce said, enthusiasm crowding her voice. "And to be frank, you don't need an architect unless you're planning to install private bathrooms for each room."

"Is that what you'd recommend?"

"Certainly not. You'd have to reduce the size of the bedrooms, and divide the existing bathrooms. It would be a shame since the structure has never been altered. You have a splendid opportunity to share Huckleberry House the way it was originally built. That doesn't happen often. I'll spend more time inspecting the place, but I don't expect to change my mind."

Neil eyed the small woman with respect. She had to know there were big bucks involved in the project, but she was turning down the work because it was the right thing to do.

"We'd like keep you on retainer," he said. "We have twelve properties so far, and some of them need more remodeling than others."

"All right."

Joyce turned immediately and pulled out her tape measure again, apparently heading for the kitchen. Neil gazed after her, fascinated. How did Libby find people like that?

"She's great," he murmured.

"I know. A while back Joyce gave us free advice on restoring the church. As my father says, she can be abrupt, but she's honest and doesn't play games."

"That's what's so great about her," Neil said. He looked at Libby and saw flickers of unhappiness in her eyes, and his gut knotted. "Hey, what's wrong?"

"Nothing."

"Like I believe that." He turned her around and marched her into the sunlight. "What gives, and don't say it's nothing."

"It's personal."

"So?"

"So we're working, and it's…personal."

"Libby, *everything* is personal when it comes to feelings," he said in exasperation. "You're the one who showed me that."

"You'll think it's silly."

"I guarantee that isn't true."

She didn't say anything for a long minute, then sighed. "Mom and Dad have refused to take any more money from me because my brother has graduated from college, the medical bills are paid off, and they say I should focus on my life. I've always been the one they counted on, and now…they don't need me any more." She shrugged.

If she hadn't told him there wouldn't be any more kissing or touching, Neil would have hugged her on the spot.

"They still need you, Libby. They'll always need you."

"But I *want* to help them. Why shouldn't I make things easier? I was already making a big salary, and now I'm making more. And it isn't as if I'm deprived, you saw my house. I can do both. Kane gives great bonuses and stock options."

Neil knew the Dumonts were trying to free Libby in more ways than just financially. They wanted her to find love and fulfillment, the way they'd found it with each other. The way his own parents had found it.

He finally understood what it was all about—love was the benchmark for everything else.

Without it, nothing else mattered.

He gave into temptation and pulled her close, wondering if she realized how perfectly she fit against his heart.

"You could do anything, Libby," he whispered, some of his own tension draining away as he absorbed her scent and warmth. "I know it seems like the ground's been ripped away from your feet, but it's still there. Just like the mountains standing around us."

Libby closed her eyes and let Neil hold her.

It did seem like solid ground wasn't there any longer, but it wasn't just because of her parents, it was because of Neil. He'd upset her world, shaken up her heart and made her want things she knew weren't possible.

Yet even knowing all that, she still felt better with him, than without him.

That evening Libby stared into the flickering light of the fire and stroked Bilbo. She was so confused. She didn't have any reason to think Neil was seeing someone else, and he truly wasn't the sort of man to court one woman and practically make love to another. On the other hand, she wasn't anything like the cool, sophisticated women he'd always dated, so it was unlikely he'd consider a permanent relationship with her.

Did he actually talk about kids and the Endicott house being a family retreat? She sighed. It would be so perfect, having a place near her parents, with all that sky and sun and meadow for gray-eyed children to play in.

"Oooh!" Libby yelped, startling Bilbo as she hit her head on the soft back of the couch, trying to knock some sense into herself.

He meowed and eyed her warily.

"Can you believe I am so stirred up about Neil O'Rourke? I would have done anything to avoid him two months ago, and now I'm thinking about babies with gray eyes and melting at the thought."

The phone rang and she grabbed it from the end table. "Hello?"

"Hi, Libby, this is Sascha."

Sascha was the real estate agent who'd sold her the house. They'd become friends after months of searching for the ideal place. "Oh. Hi, Sascha."

"You sound depressed. I suppose you've already heard the news."

Libby bolted upright. "What news?"

"Somebody just bought up all the property around the lake. I hate to say this, but it's probably a developer."

No. Her stomach churned at the idea of losing her peaceful haven. It was the only thing keeping her sane.

"But...*all* of it?"

"Yeah. I'm really sorry. We knew it was bound to happen, but I hoped it would take longer."

Great. Just great.

"I'll come over and eat ice cream with you if it helps," Sascha offered.

"No, I'm just going to drown myself in a nonfat latte," Libby said sadly. "Maybe I should have started a rumor that the lake is haunted. Do you think it's too late?"

"Probably. According to my source the buyer paid cash. I'm afraid we're looking at a real eager beaver."

Libby said goodbye and told herself that grown women didn't cry because their dream house was becoming a real estate nightmare. No big deal. Houses were just houses, and it wasn't nearly as satisfying living in her new house as she'd thought it would be.

Actually, everything was fine until Neil had stormed back into her life. So it was his fault and she shouldn't be angry because a real estate developer was going to finish the job.

The sound of a car came from the driveway and Libby sighed. She didn't want a visitor, even if it was Sascha and a carton of ice cream.

"Libby?" called a voice as a fist contacted with her door.

Neil?

Wasn't that wonderful? She'd gotten all morose

and sorry for herself earlier, and now he was present at another low point in her life. She could hide in her bedroom and pretend she wasn't there, but he was probably too smart to buy it.

Besides, it wasn't Neil's fault she'd lost her perspective. She wanted to blame him, but she'd known from the beginning what he was like—falling in love with a dedicated bachelor wasn't the brightest thing to do.

"I do have a doorbell," she said, opening the door as Neil pounded on it again. He pushed past her and she shook her head. "Please come in."

"Thanks. I need to talk to you."

"Can't it wait until tomorrow? You said you were coming back to work. We can talk at the office."

"This isn't about the office, and no, it can't wait."

Neil saw the living room was softly lit with firelight and twinkling white Christmas lights, but it wasn't dark enough to conceal Libby's pale skin. He'd hoped to have more time, to let her get used to the idea that he wanted to become a family man, but his big-mouthed realtor had taken that option away.

"I wanted to tell you I've bought the property around the lake, hopefully before anyone else let it slip."

"You're the one?" Pain and betrayal flashed in her eyes. "What do you need with so much land?"

Damn.

She'd already heard.

"*I* don't need it. I figured *we* needed it."

"Yeah, I really want to put my home in the middle of a new business development for O'Rourke Enterprises. How thrilling."

"You know me better than that," Neil said quietly.

"I bought the land because I want to keep the view from our back window as natural as possible."

Libby dropped onto the couch, looking whiter than before. "*Our* back window?"

He hitched his slacks and sat on a nearby foot rest. "That probably sounded strange. I should have started with 'I love you, and want to marry you.'"

She blinked. "You...what?"

"I love you. Please marry me."

"Marriage is a distraction, remember? It's all right for other people, but God forbid you should ever get caught in that trap—"

Neil put his hand over Libby's mouth to stop the torrent of words—something that was getting to be a habit since he used to say some dumb things.

"I know what I said, but I hoped you'd forget about it. Besides, I don't think I ever called marriage a trap. Other junk came out of my mouth about marriage, but not that one."

She stared at him mutely until he lifted his hand. Yet his thumb lingered, brushing the velvet curve of her lips.

"Listen to me," he whispered. "I love you so much I can't breathe without feeling you're a part of me. And the crazy thing is, I think I fell for you the day we met."

"That was eleven years ago."

"I know. But there were so many things I didn't understand, about myself, about my father and the decisions he made. Somewhere along the road I started believing you could either have love and a family, or a career. Then we met and you were so tempting...and I needed to think you weren't any different than other women."

"I'm not."

"Yes, you are, but not because you wouldn't sleep with me on a first date. That wouldn't have meant anything, one way or the other, though I didn't understand it at the time. I just *thought* it meant something."

Neil traced her lips again with the tip of his finger. It would be easier if she'd give him a sign, some indication of the way she felt. But at least she was listening.

"Deep down I knew you were the woman who could change my mind," he said. "Only I was too proud and too anxious to prove myself, wanting to work for my brother, but feeling I'd gotten a break that I didn't really deserve."

"You *did* deserve it."

Libby's boundless faith in people was one of the remarkable things about her, but he shook his head.

"I didn't deserve it any more than any other Harvard graduate, and somebody else wouldn't have been so cocky and full of himself. Someone else wouldn't have smugly run over everyone in his haste to show how good he was."

She smiled faintly. "Don't be too hard on yourself. I have a feeling a lot of young men want to do that."

"Run over everyone?"

"No, they want to show how good they are. But what does that have to do with me?"

Neil lifted her hands to his face, breathing kisses on them. "I met you at the wrong time, when I was too immature to understand what was really important."

"I was pretty young, too," Libby felt obliged to

point out. ''And smug in my own way. I didn't come off any better in the encounter than you did.''

''It's understandable. You were so innocent,'' he murmured. ''Scared for your mother and trying to take care of everyone, any way you could.''

''And feeling rebellious,'' she admitted. ''You don't know how close you came to winning that night.''

''Thank heaven I didn't. It wouldn't have been right for you.''

Libby blinked rapidly. Neil seemed to be offering her everything she had ever wanted, but it was so hard to be sure. She couldn't bear it if things didn't work out.

''I don't believe in the fairy tale any longer,'' she whispered. ''Can you understand that?''

''Perfectly. Both of us had to grow up sooner than we expected.'' Neil stroked her hair away from her forehead. ''But I don't want a fairy tale, Libby, I want something better. I want a wife who loves me, even if I'm not perfect. I want to work hard and take care of my family. But more than anything I just want to love you.''

When she didn't say anything, he tilted her chin up to look at him.

''Please say you love me, darling. God knows I have my faults, but I'm better because of you, and I'm sure I'll improve even faster if we spend more time together.''

Tears spilled down Libby's cheeks and she sniffed. ''You know what I was thinking in Griffith?''

''No.'' Neil dabbed at the tears tracks on her cheeks with a miserable expression on his face. ''Please don't cry. O'Rourke men don't handle it very well. I shouldn't admit that, but I know you won't use it against me.''

"I can't help it."

"All right. What were you thinking in Griffith?''

"I was thinking how I didn't believe in fairy tales, but it didn't matter, because you're better than a prince.''

His smile blazed out. "Now I know you must love me.''

"Of course I love you."

With breathtaking speed she was swept into Neil's arms and a rain of kisses fell across her face.

"Thank God, I've waited forever to hear that.''

She laughed as he tumbled both of them onto the couch. Oh, she loved his weight and strength, and everything about him. And his hands…everywhere, stroking over her hips and waist and curving around her breasts. The heat built so quickly she moaned.

"I know, love, I know.'' Neil put his hands over her head, curling them in loose fists. "I didn't mean to go right to the hard stuff—it's a long drive home and now I need another cold shower.''

Libby blushed, even as she laughed again.

"Are you always going to get that pretty pink color when I say something outrageous?'' Neil asked, grinning.

"Probably. But I plan to shock you a few times, too. You've no idea how much I enjoyed seeing you naked.''

"I invited you to watch, though I didn't really expect you to do it.''

"I can't wait for a repeat.''

"On our wedding night. I want to do things in the right order,'' Neil breathed, becoming more serious.

He dropped a kiss in the hollow of her throat. "How soon can we get married?"

"I don't care about a big wedding, so whenever you want."

"That sounds perfect." Then he groaned. "Except your mother and my mother will get together and they'll accuse me of being insensitive and unromantic if we have a quickie wedding. That sort of thing is always the groom's fault."

"What do you suggest?"

"If you don't mind getting married in January, I say we give them a month to do their worst. And that way we can plan our honeymoon. How about spending a few weeks visiting bed-and-breakfast inns, making love and checking out the competition?"

The rat.

She socked him on the arm and he chuckled.

"Just joking, sweetheart. How about the Bahamas? Warm sand, warm beach, warm water…and a very big bed."

"Hmm. You know what everyone says about you, right?"

Neil looked at her warily. "What's that?"

"They say your idea of commitment is a weekend in the Bahamas." Her mischievous smile sent warmth through his heart.

"They do, huh? I guess we could go to Alaska— this time of the year the nights last around twenty-two hours, which is just fine by me. But we spend the first night upstairs."

She looked at him quizzically. "Why?"

"Because it seems right to start our life here—and I haven't slept for days thinking about making love to you in that bedroom. I want to make our babies there, and raise them in a place that's peaceful and beautiful, like their mother.''

Libby stroked her fingers over Neil's face, marveling at the way everything had changed from dark to light. She loved him more than she'd ever imagined was possible.

''I'm not beautiful.''

''You're so beautiful it takes my breath away,'' he said, so firm and certain Libby didn't argue.

She glanced around the living room and knew it would only be home now if Neil was there. But any place could be home, it didn't have to be a place where he wasn't comfortable. ''Do you really want to live here? It's so quiet and far out of the city. You don't have to do it for me.''

''Oh, babe, I want to live here for *us*. We're going to need the lake and the quiet after a busy day. The same way we'll need the house in Endicott. I want to make love to you without feeling guilty and embarrassed because your father is down the hall.''

''Because he's a preacher.''

''Partly. Lucky me his daughter is a temptress. And an angel.''

''Hardly an angel. You've seen my temper more than anyone else alive.''

''Yup. But that's all right. I love that part of you, too. Now, do you want to call everyone and tell them the news, or do something else?''

Libby looped her arms around his neck. ''Definitely something else. I have a lot of time to make up for.''

''I was hoping you'd say that,'' Neil murmured as he gathered her close.

Epilogue

"**Y**ou don't think Libby is going to change her mind?" Neil asked as he fumbled with his tie. "She wouldn't do that, would she?"

"You're supposed to have cold feet about getting married, not whether the bride is going to show up. Though I did hear her ask for the fastest way out of town," said his sister, Shannon. She seemed to be enjoying his frenzy and he gave her a dire glance.

"That isn't funny. Libby is smart and beautiful and could marry anyone she wanted. I should never have suggested waiting a month. It gave her way too much time to reconsider."

"Libby is crazy about you and she's definitely showing up at the altar," assured Patrick. "Get out of here, Shannon. We're trying to get dressed and you're being a pain."

With a grin Shannon flipped her hand and sailed through the door. The construction company had worked miracles in the house Neil had bought as a weekend retreat, though it wasn't ready for real habitation. It was, however, sufficient for the family of the groom to use for their preparations.

The Dumonts would have happily shared their home, but Neil knew there were traditions about the groom not seeing the bride before the wedding, and he wanted everything to be perfect for Libby.

"Damn."

He yanked the tie off his neck and glared at the offending piece of fabric. He didn't really think Libby would change her mind. Not really. She was the steadfast type, and said she loved him.

"I'll do it," Kane said, taking the tie and untangling it. "You have to calm down, Neil."

"Right. With both you and Mom talking about what it means to be married and what Dad would have told me today if he only could have been here, and Shannon thinking she's a comedian, I'm going to calm down. You bet."

"Mom talked to both Patrick and me before we got married."

Patrick nodded in agreement. "Come to think of it, I was in a worse panic than you are right now." He stopped and seemed to consider something. "Well, almost worse. I didn't have to wait as long, worrying about something going wrong—I talked Maddie into a two day engagement."

Neil snorted. "Only you aren't famous for idiotic ideas about marriage and commitment. I'm not deaf, I've heard the comments. I used to think it was funny, but Libby even teased me about it, saying my idea of commitment is a weekend in the Bahamas. Libby is just so sweet, she wasn't angry at all when I suggested we go there for our honeymoon."

Kane stroked the side of his mouth. "Sweet? I seem to remember you having some good arguments in the last month."

Neil stuck his finger in his oldest brother's face. "Don't say anything bad about Libby."

"I didn't. I happen to approve of you marrying her, but you've gotten yourself in a lather for nothing. As far as Libby is concerned, you're the sun and moon and sky put together. I've seen the way she looks at you, so take some deep breaths and it'll be over before you know it."

"Yeah, right. Oh, my God. Do you think Shannon was serious about her getting out of town? *Shannon!*" Neil shouted and headed for the door in the same moment.

"Slow down." Kane hauled him around and pushed him into a chair. "Libby grew up here, so she already knows the fastest way out of town—for that matter, it's the *only* way. And if you don't cool it, you're going to have a stroke before the ceremony."

Neil knew he was overreacting, but it was hard to believe he was getting his heart's desire after wasting years chasing an illusion. How strange that he'd traveled all over the world, only to come home and find he'd mistaken money for success, and power for happiness.

"Before I forget," Kane said, pulling a small package out of his pocket, "Libby's brother just delivered this for you. Your bride-to-be wanted you to have it before going to the church."

Inside the box was a fine watch, and with a surge of anticipation Neil turned it over. Below an engraving of two linked hearts was an inscription— *My dearest love...it isn't the time we missed that counts, it's the time we have together. Some miracles are worth the wait.*

A certainty swept over him, and the tension drained away. Libby understood him better than anyone, even his family. When she loved, she loved completely, without reservation.

He put the watch on his wrist and noted the time.

"All right," he said. "It's time to go."

"Darling, it's time," said Faye Dumont, looking healthy and radiant in a pink lace dress.

Libby smiled. Neil had brought in a top heart specialist to check her mother, sweet-talking her into the examination with charm and finesse. The doctor had adjusted Faye's medication and recommended a careful regime of exercise. She was doing so much better the entire family had breathed a sigh of relief.

"I know, Mom. Go sit down." Libby took a last look at herself in the vestibule mirror, then closed her eyes for a brief prayer. She'd expected to feel nervous, yet despite the last minute wedding hysteria assailing everyone else, peace had filled her all morning.

Marrying Neil was the answer to cherished dreams and hopes, the sweet melding of childhood fantasies and adult wishes and realities. It closed a circle, and opened a new world for both of them. He'd discovered the man he was always meant to be, and she'd found freedom in his love.

Ginger, her matron of honor and only attendant, winked and disappeared into the church, walking slowly down the short aisle.

The music swelled and Libby took a long stemmed peach rose from the table, tied with a thin white satin ribbon. She hadn't wanted a fancy bouquet, but something clean and direct, like the mountains she'd grown up in.

Timothy Dumont was waiting at the sanctuary doors. "You are the loveliest bride I've ever seen, just like your mother," he said. "Ready, darling?"

Libby nodded and took her father's arm. He would officiate during the ceremony, but she'd also asked him to walk her down the aisle, like any other dad.

Though everyone stood and the church was impossibly full of their family and friends, Libby only saw Neil waiting in front of the altar, his loving, confident smile encompassing her.

It was difficult to look away from him, even to focus on the words her father was speaking. For better or worse, richer or poorer…love everlasting. The cool gold ring sliding onto her finger, the wider circlet she put on Neil's hand, all were a kaleidoscope of sound and sight and sensation. Then his arms were strong and sure around her, his kiss wiping everything else away.

Their gazes clung for an endless moment, and the vows they'd spoken were repeated and affirmed in that silent communication. Promises that would never be broken because they were written in their souls.

I love you. Neil's mouth formed the words no one else could hear at the same moment she did the same.

They both laughed, and he caught her in another kiss, more bawdy this time, more filled with heated forerunners of their coming night together.

All at once Libby and Neil were surrounded by family, hugging and kissing them, congratulating each in turn. Tears were wiped away, cheer replacing nuptial sentiment, and the party moved to Huckleberry

House, which had been cleaned and decorated for a wedding reception since it was the largest available space in Endicott.

"To the bride and groom," toasted Kane, smiling broadly as he lifted his glass. "And to the best management team in my company."

Everyone laughed as Libby blushed. Neil had insisted they become co-presidents of the division, equal partners in everything. It would be interesting. They'd already argued over a number of things, but it was fun making up, and they'd agreed to leave business at the doors of O'Rourke Enterprises.

It was wonderful knowing he'd love and accept her no matter how much they disagreed.

"Dear child, I'm so happy," said Pegeen O'Rourke, giving Libby a kiss on her cheek. "I couldn't have asked for a finer wife for my son."

"And you've been plotting it forever," teased Neil.

"What?" Confused, Libby looked between her new husband and mother-in-law.

"Mom decided ages ago that you should marry me," he explained. "She's been awfully annoyed I didn't cooperate before now."

"Anyone could have seen you were right for each other." Pegeen gave him a severe glance, a look that was spoiled by the pleasure gleaming in her eyes. "Sometimes children need a little proddin' in the right direction, remember that, Libby darlin', with your own little ones."

Warmth spun through every cell of Libby's body at the thought of carrying Neil's baby, and from the heat in his gaze, she knew he was thinking about it, as well.

"So, when *are* you going to get pregnant?" asked Shannon, handing Libby a glass of wedding punch.

"We haven't decided."

"Mom will be crushed if it isn't tonight."

"I will not," said her mother with great dignity. "And you should be thinking about startin' your own family, child, instead of teasin' your brothers."

"Me? I'm happy the way I am, thank you." Yet a faint melancholy flashed in Shannon's eyes before it was concealed, and Libby squeezed her hand. She understood. Shannon wanted to find her own Mr. Right, but he never seemed to come along.

"Don't be sad," Neil murmured as Pegeen and Shannon walked away, still affectionately arguing about Shannon's future as a mother. "She'll figure it out. Like I did."

He pressed a kiss into Libby's palm and she melted, unable to think of anything else.

"Thank you for the watch," he breathed. "It was perfect."

She sighed with pleasure.

Though snow had finally fallen and stayed in the evergreen shadows, the day was unseasonably warm and bright...which was a good thing, Libby thought, considering her dress. She smiled a secret smile and touched the spaghetti strap at her left shoulder. Neil kissed her on the very same spot and his arm slid around her tummy, sweeping her against his chest. Warmth instantly suffused her, from the nape of her neck to the back of her thighs.

"You feel so good," he breathed, nuzzling the sensitive skin at her temple. "Smell so good. And that dress..." His hand flattened over her tummy, the thin satin catching slightly on his calluses. "You nearly gave me heart failure, walking down the aisle."

"You approve, then?"

"Approve?" Neil let out a low, husky laugh. "Oh, yeah, I approve." He would never forget the way Libby had looked coming to him, a vision of innocence and sexy awareness.

Her gown was simplicity itself, a shimmering satin that draped low over her breasts, hugged her tummy and fell in soft, graceful folds from her hips. Her only adornments were a single rose, the antique crystal necklace he'd given her a few days before, and a veil of fragrance.

He didn't know if she'd chosen such a provocative wedding dress because she wanted him to forget she was a preacher's daughter, or for some other reason, but he'd take care of any concerns she had on that score. *Tonight.* Libby might be a virgin, but she was a passionate, responsive woman who desired him. The thought took his breath away. He was the luckiest man alive.

"What are you thinking about?" Libby whispered as they swayed together, his arms crossed over her waist, listening to their friends and family laugh and talk together.

"Just how happy I am. I'm glad I finally figured out what was important."

"And what's that?"

"You. Our life together." Neil turned Libby in his arms and gazed into her face. "You're the only thing I can't live without. You and our family will always come first."

"I know."

Her green eyes were shining with unqualified love

and faith, and as he drew her closer, he heard his father's voice.

I'm proud of you, son.

Neil smiled and gave Libby a kiss that was both tender and glittering with the passion to come. He loved her to the depths of his soul, and this was only the beginning.

*   *   *   *   *

SILHOUETTE *Romance*®

ONE BACHELOR TO GO
by Nicole Burnham
(Silhouette Romance #1706)

I did it! I married off the bachelor executives at the company before my dad, the boss, forced them to court me. Well, only gorgeous, super-successful VP Jack Devon is left. But who in the world would make the perfect match for the frustratingly private man? Certainly not me...right?

—Emily Winters, the boss's daughter

Don't miss the final heartwarming story this February 2004 in the fun-filled series from Silhouette Romance,

Marrying The Boss's Daughter

With office matchmakers on the loose, is any eligible executive safe?

Available February 2004 at your favorite retail outlet.

Visit Silhouette at www.eHarlequin.com   SROBTG

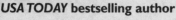

SILHOUETTE *Romance* ®

Presents

Two terrific new titles in

Patricia Thayer's

THE TEXAS BROTHERHOOD

Cheated of their Randell birthright,
and now reunited with the brothers who
bear their father's name, two rugged
cowboys create a legacy of their own....

Don't miss either episode
in this powerful family saga!

WYATT'S READY-MADE FAMILY
(Silhouette Romance #1707, On Sale February 2004)

DYLAN'S LAST DARE
(Silhouette Romance #1711, On Sale March 2004)

Available at your favorite retail outlet.

If you enjoyed what you just read,
then we've got an offer you can't resist!

Take 2 bestselling
love stories FREE!

Plus get a FREE surprise gift!

eHARLEQUIN.com

The eHarlequin.com online community is *the* place to share opinions, thoughts and feelings!

- Joining the community is easy, fun and **FREE!**

- Connect with **other romance fans** on our message boards.

- Meet your **favorite authors** without leaving home!

- **Share opinions** on books, movies, celebrities…and *more!*

Here's what our members say:

"I love the friendly and helpful atmosphere filled with support and humor."
—Texanna (eHarlequin.com member)

"Is this the place for me, or what? There is nothing I love more than 'talking' books, especially with fellow readers who are reading the same ones I am."
—Jo Ann (eHarlequin.com member)

Join today by visiting www.eHarlequin.com!

SILHOUETTE *Romance*®

COMING NEXT MONTH

#1706 ONE BACHELOR TO GO—Nicole Burnham
Marrying the Boss's Daughter

Emily Winters had successfully married off all of her dad's eligible executives except one: Jack Devon, the devilishly handsome VP of Global Strategy. A business trip was her chance to learn more about the man behind the mysterious demeanor. But after sharing close quarters—and a few passionate kisses—Emily was ready to marry Jack off…
to herself!

#1707 WYATT'S READY-MADE FAMILY—
Patricia Thayer
The Texas Brotherhood

When rodeo rider Wyatt Gentry came face-to-face with sassy single mom Maura Wells, she was holding a rifle on him! The startled, sexy cowboy soon convinced her to put down the gun and give him a job on her ranch. Now if he could only convince the love-wary beauty that he was the man who could teach her and her two kids how to trust again.…

#1708 FLIRTING WITH THE BOSS—Teresa Southwick
If Wishes Were…

Everybody should have money and power, right? But despite her birthday wish, all that Ashley Gallagher got was Max Bentley, her boss's heartbreaker of a grandson. She had to convince him to stay in town long enough to save the company. And love-smitten Ashley was more than ready to use any means necessary to see that Max stayed put!

#1709 SAVED BY THE BABY—Linda Goodnight

Julianna Reynolds would do anything to save her dying daughter—even ask Sheriff Tate McIntyre to father another child. Trouble was, she'd never told him about their *first* child! Shocked, Tate would only agree to her plan if Julianna became his wife. But could their new baby be the miracle they needed to save their daughter *and* their marriage of convenience?

SRCNM0104